By my Side

A SECOND WORLD WAR LOVE STORY

SUE REID

■SCHOLASTIC

60000312280

While the events described and some of the characters in this book may
be based on actual historical events and real people, this story is a work
of fiction.

Scholastic Children's Books
Euston House, 24 Eversholt Street,
London, NW1 1DB, UK

A division of Scholastic Ltd
London ~ New York ~ Toronto ~ Sydney ~ Auckland
Mexico City ~ New Delhi ~ Hong Kong

Published in the UK by Scholastic Ltd, 2014

Text copyright © Sue Reid, 2014
Cover photography copyright © Jeff Cottenden, 2014

ISBN 978 1407 13896 1

Printed and bound by CPI Group UK (ltd), Croydon, CR0 4YY

2 4 6 8 10 9 7 5 3 1

The right of Sue Reid and Jeff Cottenden to be identified as the author
and cover photographer of this work has been asserted by them in
accordance with the Copyright, Designs and Patents Act, 1988.

AMSTERDAM, 1942

7 JANUARY 1942

I'm not sure this is the usual way to start a diary. Not that I've ever kept one before. Anneke does. Once I asked her what she wrote in it. "Things I can't tell anyone," she said, rather too promptly. I felt a bit hurt when she said that. But now I feel I understand. Sometimes there are things you can't tell anyone. Not even your best friend. Something that you know might turn into something big. And you just know when that happens. And it can happen in the most ordinary, unsurprising way, on a day that begins like any other – like today.

After school Maarten and I cycled home. I'd been quite flattered that he wanted to accompany me. He's the cleverest boy in the class – and he said he'd help me with my maths homework. Saskia – who sits on one side of me at school, Anneke sits on the other – says that's because he likes me, but she would. Saskia is boy-mad. I'm not – I like lots of things.

We hadn't gone far when we began to quarrel. Maarten's a bit of a know-it-all. But isn't it strange how things happen? If we hadn't been quarrelling we'd not have taken the wrong turning and I'd never have met Jan.

I only realized that we'd missed the turning when we found ourselves at Mr Breitkopf's shop. Only we could hardly see it for all the people standing in front of it. Maarten said we should go, but I wanted to find out what was happening. I'm nosier I suppose. Besides, I like Mr Breitkopf. Then the tall man in front of us moved aside and I could see old Mr B, his face terrified, cowering in his doorway. Some boys were jumping up and down, taunting him. "Jood. Jood." That wasn't all. Men wearing the uniforms of the Dutch police were watching them, grinning, arms folded. They did nothing to stop the boys. It made me feel sick. Let me be plain. Most of my countryfolk are good, decent people, but some belong to the Dutch Nazi party. And the Occupation has made them bold.

"You've got to do something," I hissed to Maarten.

He looked at me as if I was mad.

"What can I do?" he said.

"Stop them! He might get hurt."

"I can't!"

"Someone's got to!" I'd raised my voice and one or two people turned round and stared at me.

"No, I can't," he said again.

I looked at him. His face had gone red.

And then I understood. I felt a bit sick. It was as if he'd said aloud: "Because he's a Jew."

"Then I will!"

He grabbed at my arm. "Don't be stupid. They'll kill you!"

I shook him off. "Now you're being stupid!" I said. "They're only boys." I'd forgotten about the police.

"Katrien!"

"Oh go away, you coward." I pushed him away, wishing I felt as brave as I'd sounded. I was scared – truly scared. What did I think I was doing? A hateful little voice was whispering in my head: *Maarten's right, you know. Go home. It's none of your business.*

I'd nearly reached the front of the group when I heard a voice shout "No!" and I looked up to see a boy throw himself in front of the old man. There was a vicious crump and I saw the boy reel backwards, his hand held to his face. Blood was seeping through his fingers. "That will teach you to help a Jew!" a harsh voice growled. His fist drew back to strike again. That was enough for me!

"Stop it!" I shouted. "Stop!" My voice sounded very thin to my ears, but the man put up his fist and swung round. You should have seen his face. A girl – standing up to the police. It seemed to rouse the people near me. One man hastily hauled the boy to his feet, and another helped Mr B away. I stared back as bravely as I could, a vision of my soon-to-be-bloodied face like a mirror in front of my eyes. But to my surprise I heard the policeman laugh, his friend said "come on", and they slunk away like bored dogs to find someone else to torment. I thanked whoever was watching out for me for my lucky escape.

Then I ran up to the boy. He was leaning against the shop, his hand over his mouth. "Are you all right?" I said.

"You should thank this girl, lad," said the man who'd helped him. "You'd have got worse if she hadn't stepped in. You're very brave," he added to me.

"I know," the boy said through his fingers.

"Not as brave as you," I said – all the compliments making me feel rather embarrassed. The boy gave me a lopsided smile. The eyes he turned on me were startlingly blue. Not many people have eyes that blue. And it was that I think that made me feel sure I'd seen him before somewhere. I just couldn't think where.

The boy took his hand from his face and spat out some blood. His mouth was swelling fast.

I turned my head away. Looking at that face was making me feel a bit sick. I fished in my pocket for my hanky.

"Here," I said, handing it to him, "take this. It's quite clean," I added.

"Thank you," the boy said, taking it from me and gingerly mopping his mouth. I saw him wince. It must have hurt.

"That mouth needs seeing to," I said.

"Are you a doctor?" the boy said, his voice muffled through the hanky. I felt he was trying to make a joke and I was impressed that he was able to.

"My father's a doctor," I said. "He'll look at it for you." I put my hand lightly on his arm to encourage him. All the people who'd been watching had wandered away now, but the streets were far from quiet and we were getting some pretty funny looks. I knew I had to get him away. He couldn't stay there – not with a face like that.

He shook his head. "I'll be all right."

"It's not far," I promised. "I only want to help," I added, when he still looked doubtful.

He nodded. "OK." He held out his hand, saw it was bloodied and hastily withdrew it. "I'm Jan," he said. And it was as if something clicked in my memory and I knew that I had seen him before. At my school. I didn't really know him – only in the way younger girls know of older boys. He wasn't one of the boys girls hung around. But when I told him my name I could see it meant nothing to him, so I didn't say anything about school.

We hadn't gone far when Jan stopped and put a hand on my arm. "What's wrong?" I asked. I glanced at his face. It was deathly pale.

"Can't you see them?" he whispered.

"Who?"

"Soldiers!"

"What?"

"Over by the railings."

Then I saw them. And I saw that they'd seen us.

I knew it was bad. They'd ask for our identity cards. I was used to this. It's part of living under Nazi Occupation. It had never worried me before. I'd hand over my card, they'd look at it, then at me, and hand it back. But this time it would be different. This time there would be questions. "*How did you come by that face, hein? You were in a fight? There was trouble at a Jew's shop today. We are looking for a girl and a boy. His injuries match yours.*" They'd take him away. And maybe me, too. And there was nothing I could do about it. And it was then I had this extraordinary feeling. That my brief act of courage was going to turn my world upside down.

"Run?" I suggested, as if Jan was able to.

"Too late," he muttered.

I looked over to see that one of the soldiers had already detached himself from the group and was walking towards us. Jan pressed the hanky back over his face to try and hide his injured mouth. The hanky was all bloody, though. He might as well not have bothered.

"You have been in a fight?" the soldier said as he reached us.

Jan was silent. So was I.

The German was waiting. One of us had to say something. But what?

"Maybe he fights over you? Your boyfriend." The German grinned. It wasn't what I'd expected him to say and to my annoyance I felt myself blush. I couldn't tell what Jan thought – I didn't dare look at him.

"You are a very pretty girl," the soldier said.

I was disgusted. He was our enemy. Did he think I cared what he thought?

"Cigarette?" The soldier took a pack from his pocket and held one out to me.

I gave him a cold stare. "I don't smoke."

"No?"

"I'm a schoolgirl."

"Ah, I see." My reply had disconcerted him. He'd taken me for an older girl.

"Well, maybe then…" His eyes turned from me back to Jan. They narrowed.

I felt a moment's panic. It was coming, the German was going to take him away, and I'd not be able to stop him. I looked around. There were plenty of people in the street, but if they saw the desperation in my face they ignored it. I couldn't blame them. Who would want to step in and put themselves in danger? Over by the railings the German soldiers were prowling, like a pack of dogs who'd smelt blood. Any minute now…

"Katrien?" I swung round to see our neighbour, Mrs Meier, staring at us. My relief at seeing a friendly face was so great I nearly burst into tears. If anyone could get us out of this mess she would. She didn't waste time asking for explanations but marched straight up to the soldier. "Officer," she said. "I must get these children home."

Children! I'm nearly sixteen!

But for once I'd enough sense to keep what I thought to myself.

"You know them?" the German said, putting the cigarettes away in his pocket.

"I do," she said, though I felt sure she had never seen Jan before. I found myself praying he wouldn't ask her for our names.

"I see that I have made a mistake." But I saw in his eyes that he knew. No mistake. But for some reason he was letting us go. I tried not to think it had anything to do with me.

He glanced at me again. For a moment his eyes held mine. Then he smiled. "Take him home. His face needs cleaning up." He nodded and sauntered back to his friends. The soldiers seemed to settle. I heard one of them laugh.

Mrs Meier put a firm hand on each of our shoulders to lead us away. "Hurry," she said. Not that we needed urging. The soldiers were still lingering by the railings.

"Thank you," Jan said. "I am very grateful. But I must go now."

"Don't try to talk," she said quietly.

She doesn't want to know. She is wise.

It was only a short walk to our house. While Mrs Meier rang the doorbell, I waited on the steps with Jan. My stomach was bouncing around inside me. What was Mother going to say when she saw him? How would I explain where I'd been? Jan was looking up at the house. Suddenly I saw how it might look to a stranger. The narrow imposing house, gazing out on to the frozen canal. A house where well-to-do people live. The leafless trees, their bare branches reaching up to embrace the sky. Children, well wrapped up, sliding down the canal. The people walking slowly by its side – I saw how prosperous they looked, even now. I saw then how thin Jan's coat and scarf were. He swallowed. Was he nervous, too? I touched his hand to reassure him. He glanced at me and I saw again how blue his eyes were. Blue eyes and dark hair. I like that. It's unusual.

"Katrien?" I looked up to see that the door of our house had opened. Mother was standing there, staring at me. "Where have you been? I've been so worried." And then she saw Jan.

I don't think I'll ever forget the expression on her face.

His face was swelling nicely and there was dried blood on one cheek.

"Why! Who is this? Whatever has happened?" she got out at last.

"I found these two on the street," said Mrs Meier swiftly, popping round from behind us. "And the young man needs help. Margrit, I'll see you tomorrow. Goodnight, children." With a quick bob of her head she was gone.

"Perhaps you will explain, Katrien," Mother said. I'd pulled Jan in behind me before she could object. "Who is this, and where is Maarten?" She glanced back as if she half expected to see him lurking behind us.

I sought for something to say. "Mother, this is Jan – a boy at my school." I saw Jan's start of surprise, and I hurried on before he could say anything. "He got hurt defending Mr Breitkopf from some Dutch Nazis!"

"Oh, no!" she exclaimed. "The poor old man! Is he all right?"

"Yes," I said. "He got away."

Mother turned back to Jan. "You are a brave boy! Sit down – please – and take off your coat and scarf. I'll give your face a bathe. My husband can take a proper look at it when he gets back."

"I don't want to be any trouble," Jan said. I could sense how uncomfortable he was. His eyes wandered around the hall, staring at it. At the fine clock, the polished hall table.

"It's no trouble." A smile wavered briefly on her face. "Katrien, come with me."

Leaving Jan standing there, I followed Mother into the kitchen. I watched while she ran warm water into a bowl. Her back to me she said, "Katrien, I don't understand. Who is this boy? You've never mentioned him before. And what is this about Dutch Nazis?"

I felt as if I was being cross-examined. I seized on the one question I could safely answer. "They were bullying Mr Breitkopf and Jan stepped in."

"And Jan – what do you know about him?"

"He goes to my school." Or he did. A slight suspicion was

forming in my mind, but I kept it to myself. I wasn't even sure I was right.

"Don't be silly, Katrien. You know what I mean. Who is he? Who are his people?"

"I've told you all I know. Anyway, does it matter?"

"Don't speak to me like that, Katrien."

"Well, didn't I do the right thing bringing him home? You always say we should help when we can!"

"I hope so," she said quietly. "I hope so." She turned to me. "And Maarten? Where is he?"

I shrugged. "I don't know. Probably run home to hide. He's a coward, Mother. He didn't even try to help." I remembered the expression on Maarten's face. I didn't like thinking about it. He hadn't helped him because he was a Jew.

"He's not a coward. Katrien, what could he do?" She sighed. "Don't be too hard on him. He's a nice boy."

I don't think he is, Mother. Not as nice as you think.

"Now we must go back to Jan." I followed her back into the hallway where Jan was waiting. He had taken off his coat and scarf, but he looked as if he wished he was a million miles away. I saw Mother try to smile as she dabbed water on his face. She told him again that he was brave, but I felt that she wished he was miles away, too. I saw how relieved she was when the front door opened and Father came in. He examined Jan's face carefully. "Nothing is broken," he said. "You've been lucky, young man. So," he said when he'd finished, "how did you come by this injury? It's a nasty one."

I opened my mouth to speak, but Father shook his head at me. "Let the lad speak for himself, Katrien."

"I was trying to protect Mr Breitkopf," he said. He shrugged as if protecting Jewish people was something he did every day.

"You're a brave boy," Father said, putting a hand on Jan's shoulder. "It is shameful what is happening. Shameful."

They went on and on about how shameful it was. I wished they'd stop. Couldn't they tell how uncomfortable they were making him? "I'd better go," he said at last, shifting from foot to foot. "My parents will be wondering where I am."

They offered him tea, food, but Jan refused it all. Even cake! Fancy refusing cake!

I went with him to the door. I was hoping he'd say something like: I'll see you at school, Katrien. Or: maybe I can walk you home tomorrow. But he didn't. Maybe it was just that my parents were standing nearby, breathing over us like dragons. Not that they needed to. I knew he was a nice respectful boy. I can't explain how I knew. I just did. Like you do.

It was only after he'd gone that I saw it. His scarf, lying on the floor. He must have dropped it in his haste to leave. I picked it up and ran outside. I looked up and down the street. But of course he'd gone.

I've folded it up and put it on the chair so I won't forget it in the morning. It's pretty moth-eaten, lots of little holes in it. Mother would say it's only fit for the bin. I'll take it to school tomorrow and give it to him then. Maybe he'll be so pleased he'll walk me home.

8 JANUARY

I'm writing in an old school exercise book. It's lucky I found it, or I wouldn't be able to keep a diary. Paper's in short supply, like so many other things in Holland now. I'm squashing as many words on to the page as I can, to make it last. My brother, Pieter, says my writing looks as if a spider had fallen into an inkpot and crawled across the page! He has a nerve. His is no better.

I've found a place to hide it – under the mattress. It's pretty lumpy, so no one will know it's there even if they accidentally sit down on it.

I've pulled the eiderdown up to my chin. It's freezing! Heating is another thing that's rationed, and the house is always cold. Mother *says* she turns it up in the living room in the evening but even if you sit on the radiator it feels barely warm at all.

But at least I feel full for once. Mrs Meier came round for tea. She brought some of her home-made biscuits. Pieter wasn't home, so I ate his share as well as mine. Mrs Meier's biscuits are famous! She encouraged me to eat up. "You're a growing girl," she said. Mother said if I go on like that I'll grow outwards as well as upwards. Mrs Meier just laughed. She's really nice. She asked after Jan, too. I told her I hadn't seen him. I expect his mother's kept him home, she said, but I saw the glance that passed between Mother and her.

I had to go to school on foot this morning. I couldn't find my bike. It was only when I was halfway there that I remembered where I'd left it. Outside Mr Breitkopf's shop. I felt like kicking myself. Someone would almost certainly have stolen it, and how would I confess to Mother and Father? It had been their present to me on my fifteenth birthday. I asked Pieter if I could borrow his, but he was annoyed that I'd woken him, and grunted that he needed it to get to university, before turning over on his side and going back to sleep again. My brother is so lazy. He'd stay in bed all day if Mother let him.

Of course by then I was late so I had to run all the way. As I dashed through the school gates I saw Maarten over by the bike racks. I pretended I hadn't seen him but he saw me and waved me over. Then I saw what was propped up next to him. My bike! I was so relieved but he wouldn't let me thank him, just shoved the bike at me and stalked off. Not that I care. I don't want to be friends with him any more. He let me down. I think he feels the same – for when I got into the classroom I saw that he'd moved his books to sit as far from me as he could without falling out of the window. As we were putting our books away at the end of the lesson Saskia leant across to ask what was up between us. I didn't tell her, of course. You don't tell Saskia anything unless you want everyone to know. She cannot keep a secret.

I looked out for Jan at school but I didn't see him – not once. Several times I thought I had but each time the boy turned round I realized my mistake. After a time I had to stop. I was getting some pretty funny looks. Mrs Meier must be right. His mother will have kept him at home. I'll try again tomorrow.

9 JANUARY

Maarten actually spoke to me today. He asked how I was getting on with my maths homework. He smiled, but it wasn't a very nice smile. I didn't answer him. At lunch he disappeared somewhere with Saskia. He made sure I saw, too. As if I care!

Later Anneke came over to perch on my desk. She asked

me what was wrong between us. I shrugged and said we'd fallen out. "Why?" she asked.

"We quarrelled, Anneke, that's all," I said doodling with my pen on my exercise book so she couldn't see my face. She must guess that I'm holding something back but I don't want to talk about it – not even to my best friend. I'm finding out just what a friend a diary can be. You can write what you like and it will never ask awkward questions!

I've still got Jan's scarf. I'm wondering what to do with it. It's too worn for me to wear, but I don't want to throw it away. I looked on the timetable this morning to find out what classes he's in so that I could wait for him afterwards, but there are lots of older boys called Jan. Then I thought of stationing myself at the gate at the end of school to see if I could catch him then, but Anneke and Saskia were with me.

Maybe his family are keeping him at home for a few days. I've just got to be patient.

12 JANUARY

After school today I cycled over to Mr Breitkopf's shop. I don't know what drew me back there. I suppose I was curious to see it again. It's not his shop now, of course.

Jewish businesses have been taken away from their owners and given to new ones. I heard Father talk about it. It's one more way the Nazis have found to torment the Jews. They've become very good at that.

I propped my bike up against a railing and walked over to the shop. I wondered what he'd been doing there that day, poor old man.

In the old days before the War began and spoilt everything Mother often used to bring me here. It was a treasure trove of all sorts of curious and wonderful things. I loved exploring it. When Mother was being served Mr B used to slip me sweets from out of a big glass jar he kept on one of the shelves at the back. It makes me feel sad to think about that. The shop was closed for the day and the door was locked so I went up to a window and peered in. It looked musty and untidy as if no one had been there for a long time. Whoever owns it now isn't looking after it.

I got back on my bike and cycled away. I've been thinking a lot about Mr B. I wonder how he's managing now. It can't be easy for him. I doubt the Nazis gave him a fair price for the shop. More likely they just stole it.

13 JANUARY

We have extra German classes now. It's one of the new laws our Nazi masters have brought in to try and turn us into good little Nazis. It won't work, of course – any more than anything else they've tried. They were very friendly when they first occupied our country. *Hey, we like your country. That's why we invaded it! Aren't you pleased? No? Why not?* Hardly anyone makes an effort in our German class now – except Maarten, of course. I used to think this was because he wants to be best at everything, but now I wonder if it's because he secretly admires our German masters and wants to be like them. It's an uncomfortable thought, and I hope I'm wrong. Anneke and I never make any effort, of course. This morning, I opened my English book and we spent the whole lesson passing it back and forth, concealed inside our German translation. It amuses us to think how annoyed the Nazis would be if they knew.

I wouldn't mind if they'd ban maths! In our lesson today the teacher told me he'd suggest private tuition if he thought it'd do any good! He said it in front of the whole class, too. I felt as if he was deliberately setting out to humiliate me as he went over my workings. He even turned the book upside down to see if it made more sense that way! Anneke said I should take no notice. He's just mean, no one likes him, who cares about maths anyway and I'm good at lots of things. Like a best friend should. I know she wanted me to feel better, though it's a bit of a struggle to think what those things are. Mother says I'm untidy, and Pieter says I walk around with my eyes shut. But it made me feel even meaner that I was keeping a secret from Anneke. I don't know why I feel it is important I keep Jan secret. I just do.

After school was over I saw Maarten leave hand-in-hand with Saskia. Anneke says they've started going round together. Saskia's welcome to him. I haven't told Anneke my suspicions about him. I'd rather not think that we might have a fledgeling Nazi in our class. She asked if I'd like to join her and some other friends who were going to see a new film. It's an age since I've been to the cinema, so I did. I wish I hadn't. It was awful. I'd forgotten how bad the films are now they've been censored by the Nazis. Then just before it started a whole lot of soldiers came in and sat down in the row behind us and put their feet up on the seats. Of course no one dared to object. Anneke told me afterwards that she had a boot in her back all the way through.

Usually they put on a newsreel first. It's always propaganda, like what they write on posters and paste all round the town. About how wonderful the German Reich is and how brilliantly the War is going (if you're German). But this was something else. It was called "The Eternal Jew" and the lies it told made me feel really sick. The soldiers whistled and hooted but an old couple in front of us got up in disgust. But would you believe it? They were made to sit down again!

As soon as the main film began the soldiers began to talk. If I'd dared I'd have turned round and told them to be quiet. They act as if they own my country – and can behave just as they like. I felt really upset as we left. Anneke and I have made a pact now – no more films till the Germans are defeated.

I got home just in time to hear the daily broadcast from the BBC in London. I'd have been furious if I'd missed that on top of everything else. Each evening we're at home – which is nearly every evening these days – we settle down in comfy chairs around the radio. At eight o'clock Father switches it on and we listen out for the peep peep peep which tells us that the broadcast from London is about to begin. Of course it's against the Nazis' laws to listen to it, but no one takes any notice. We have a rule in our house that no one says a word till it is over. It's the only news we can rely on. When the news is glum – which it nearly always is these days – it comforts me to think that up and down the country there are countless families listening like us. We're all longing for news of the Allies Second Front, but it's being an awful long time in coming. But tonight, after seeing all those lies about the Jews I was desperate to hear something cheerful. Father asked why the long face, so I told him. He took my hands in his and said seriously that he was sure I knew it was all lies. I nodded. I just wish they wouldn't show it. There was a little question in Father's eyes, and I think I know why. It's as if drip by drip they're pouring propaganda into us to turn us against each other, but Father needn't worry about me. All that showing that film has done has made me hate the Nazis worse than ever, and made me determined to show the Jews by any means I can that I am on their side.

14 JANUARY

I'm an idiot! It's obvious why I haven't seen Jan at school. He's Jewish. There used to be a lot of Jewish boys and girls in my school, but they had to leave last September and go to separate Jewish schools. When we went back to school in the autumn it felt strange to see how our class had shrunk. The teachers tried to make it less obvious by taking out empty desks and chairs, but there was room to stretch out properly in the classroom, which there hadn't been before. I never see my Jewish friends now. At first I used to wonder what happened to them. Then I gradually forgot. Like you do. You get on with things. It's not that I don't care. But what choice do you have? Now, having seen that film, I wish I had made more of an effort. I suppose I didn't truly understand how bad things must be for them.

I don't suppose I'll ever see Jan again, and that makes me feel a bit sad. There are so many things I'd like to ask him – and now I never will. But I'm hanging on to that scarf – as a keepsake of a special day. It will always remind me of him.

15 JANUARY

I've found out that I was right. Jan *is* Jewish. Yesterday I put his scarf away, sure that I'd never see him again. Then today I did! I've Mother to thank for that. I'm not sure she'd be pleased if she knew that, though. At least that's what Jan thinks and I've not yet managed to change his mind. I'd gone out to buy potatoes. Mother had forgotten to buy them earlier, and as it was our maid's half-day off I was sent out for them. It was quite late by then, and I had to go into a few shops before I found one that had any left. The shopkeeper weighed them out for me. Even these weren't very nice – one or two felt quite soft and had sprouty bits in them. I knew what Mother would say when she saw those so I tried to hand them back but the shopkeeper reminded me that potatoes were rationed and anyway that was all he had left. They weren't any cheaper either! It was just after I'd paid that I saw Jan. I just felt that he was there – like you do about people sometimes. I swung round and there he was.

"Katrien!" he said.

"Jan!" I said. We were staring at each other as if we were beings from another planet. I'd thought I'd never see him again, and he was looking at me as if he felt the same. There was a faint bruise on his cheek but otherwise you'd not have known the battering his face had taken.

Then I realized I was staring and dropped my eyes, but he gave me a smile – a slow smile that began on his lips and ended in his eyes. It was quite an exciting smile. I smiled back – not just a little smile, a big smile, the kind of smile you can't hold back. Then I felt embarrassed and couldn't think what to say, until I remembered that I had his scarf. When I told him, he said he'd forgotten where he'd left it, but he looked rather awkward so I wasn't sure I believed him.

I told him I'd go and get it, but he said it was too late.

"It's not too late," I said.

"It is for me," he replied.

And then, bang on cue, the clock at the end of the square struck.

I don't know if there are special curfews for Jews but it was then I felt sure that I was right. "Jan, you're Jewish, aren't you?" I said. I added quickly, before he could answer: "I don't care if you are. You're really brave and – and I like you."

I felt my cheeks go bright red. Why had I said that? Anneke would roll her eyes and say I'd been really forward, and that now I'd never see him again. But then if I hadn't said anything I probably wouldn't have either. If that makes sense.

If my face was red, his was even redder. Now I'd gone and embarrassed him.

"I like you, too, Katrien," he mumbled.

He could just be being polite. Because of what I said. But maybe he means it. Maybe he really does?

Anyway, we've arranged to meet tomorrow – I know it's only so I can give him his scarf, but I'm pleased. I suggested he meet me at my home, but he doesn't want to do that. Then I said I'd meet him at his school, but he said it's in the Jewish Quarter, and it might be better to meet outside it. How do I manage to put my foot in it? I do – every time. I've walked past the Jewish Quarter loads of times. Last year, after all the disturbances, the Nazis put up a big fence to close it off from all the rest of us. It was as high as a man standing on another man's head. They put barbed wire round it, too – just to make sure no one would try to climb out. It was awful. They've taken that all away now, but they left the notices they'd put up: "Juden Viertel" and "Joodsche Wijk" – in German and Dutch – so that everyone knows it's a Jewish neighbourhood. The Nazis are good at thinking up things like that to humiliate the Jews.

I'm looking forward to seeing him again. It is exciting to think I might have made a new friend. Even – maybe… No, it's too soon to think about things like that. Katrien, you hardly know the boy!

Must stop writing now. Mother's calling. Supper's ready.

16 JANUARY

I've a lot to write – and I hardly know where to start. I feel as if I've embarked on an adventure and I'm not sure where it will lead me. It's exciting! And if I'm honest, a bit frightening. Jan is right. It won't be easy for us to be friends. Not now. And I want us to be friends. I've never met anyone as brave as Jan. It may sound extraordinary, but it's only just sunk in. If those policemen had found out that he was Jewish, he'd have been in a lot worse trouble.

He didn't say why it would be difficult, of course, and he didn't need to. I'm not going to let myself think about it either – in case he changes his mind. I tell myself, who will care? I'm fifteen and he's seventeen. We're both still at school. No one will mind. I'm trying to believe it.

We met outside the Jewish Quarter, by the big church near the entrance. I got there first. I tried not to look at those awful signs, but my eyes were drawn to them in spite of myself. No doubt that's the point of them. Not that all Jewish people are kept inside, or us out. I saw lots of people going in and out. I even recognized some of them – girls and boys who'd been pupils at my school till September. They were chatting with their friends, just like I do with mine, as if nothing had changed. I nearly went up to them, but I couldn't think what I'd say. I hadn't kept up my friendships with them, after all. But I think that's why I felt it would be all right for Jan and me to be friends.

I was still miles away in my mind when I heard Jan's voice. I jumped and felt my cheeks go red.

To cover my embarrassment, I dug into my bulging satchel for his scarf. I'd had quite a job fitting it in along with my books.

I couldn't get it out! When I tugged all that happened was that a few books fell out, and a bit of wool got caught on the clasp. Jan picked up the books for me while I tried to untangle the wool. That just made it worse. My fingers and thumbs seemed to have grown to the size of hams. I'm not usually so clumsy.

"Here, let me," Jan said. He gave me the books and I handed him the satchel. I felt such an idiot. What must he think of me?

He untangled it easily and wound the scarf around his neck.

"Thanks for keeping it safe for me." He gave me another of those smiles that make you want to smile back. I felt grateful to him for not minding and making me feel all right about myself.

After that neither of us seemed to know quite what to say. I wanted him to say something, but I think he wanted me to. We looked at each other.

Then we both spoke at once.

"Um…"

"Er…"

"Yes?" I got in quickly before he asked what I was going to say. I hadn't really known what to say anyway.

"Er… I was going to ask if, can I er … um … walk you back?"

I saw his eyes were fixed on the church – he couldn't look me in the eye.

"Yes, that would be all right."

I had to wheel my bicycle while he walked by my side. I noticed that he kept glancing at it. I'm not surprised. It is pretty special, painted in bright green. I'd searched for damage after I'd got it back, but found only one tiny scratch.

"That's a fine bike," he said.

"It was a birthday present," I said. Then before I could stop myself I added: "Where's yours?" Most people ride bikes, it's the best way of getting round the city.

He was silent.

I felt like kicking myself. Were Jews even allowed to own bikes now? I didn't know. There was a lot I didn't know. Pieter says I walk around with my eyes half shut. Maybe he's right.

"Someone stole it," he said at last. "But anyway…" He shrugged, as if it didn't matter. But it did.

I tried to think what to say. "Well, would you like to ride mine? We could go to the park." It's quiet in the park at this time of year.

He just looked at me.

I should keep my mouth shut. Would be better if I did. I'd done it again. He couldn't ride in the park. Public parks had been forbidden to Jews since last year. The Nazis brought that restriction in just before summer – exactly when people would want to go there. I remember one of Mother's Jewish friends being upset that she couldn't take her children there any more. And now I'd gone and rubbed it in. I kicked at a stone angrily.

Then I heard him say: "It's probably too small for me anyway."

I felt all warm inside. I knew he'd said that just to make me feel better, when it was me who should be making him feel better. Jan was a nice boy. I tried to think how I could make amends.

"Why don't you try it and see?" I said. I held it out to him.

"So long as you don't laugh."

"I won't."

I did, of course. Jan towers over me by at least a foot. When he sat on the saddle his knees came almost up to his chin.

"Hey – I told you not to laugh!" he said.

He got off and we walked along together. Jan has a long stride but he shortened it so I could keep up. I walked as slowly as I could. I wanted to spin out our walk as long as I could, but I couldn't help noticing how nervous he seemed. He kept glancing around. In the end I told him to stop – he was making me nervous, too. He said he didn't realize he was doing it. "I don't often walk with Gentile girls," he told me.

It felt strange to hear him say that. I never stop to think if anyone is Jewish or a Gentile, or anything else. Even now. Other things matter to me much more.

As we walked, Jan told me a bit about himself. He lives with his family in a flat outside the Jewish Quarter and it's quite a way from his home to his school. It's a large flat, he said, but they've let out some rooms so it's a bit of a squash. I wonder if they need the money? I could tell from looking at him that money was tight. His trousers were too short for him and his shirt collar was frayed.

He's got a younger sister, called Ilse. She doesn't go to the same school. Maths is his best subject! I told him it was my worst! He asked what I liked best. I said I wasn't clever, like him.

"But you're brave, determined and resourceful," he said quietly.

I mumbled something about he was, too. It was a good thing he wasn't looking at me, for my face felt as if it was on fire. It was the nicest compliment anyone had ever paid me.

When we reached the end of my street I saw Jan hesitate.

"We're almost here. Why don't you come in?" I said.

He looked at me.

"I'm sure they'd like to see you again," I added hopefully.

"I don't know, Katrien."

"They wouldn't mind…"

"I'd rather not, if you don't mind. They … well, I didn't tell them about myself. I…"

"They'd understand."

He shook his head.

I couldn't think what else to say so I held out my hand.

"Goodbye then." We shook hands, very politely. I felt sad. It was probably the last time I'd ever see him. I'd felt that what had happened outside Mr Breitkopf's shop had made a bond between us. But maybe he didn't feel the same. Yet, he was still standing there… I heard him clear his throat.

"Actually…" he said. He shuffled a bit with his foot. "If you like, I could help you with your maths," he said quickly. His cheeks had gone a bit pink. "I'd like to be able to thank you somehow for … for what you did."

It wasn't what I'd hoped he'd say. But I was pleased all the same, even if it was only to help me with my sums.

As I pushed open the front door I could tell he was still nervous – as if facing my parents would need a lot more courage than standing up to Nazi bullies.

He needn't have worried though. No one was home. Not even my brother. I've no idea what Pieter's up to half the time. There was a note from Mother on the hall table, saying she was at a neighbour's, and to help myself to what I wanted. Father was still at the surgery. So I raided the kitchen for food, then we went into the living room and I served up tea. In proper china, too. It was fun. We didn't get very far with the maths. I found it hard to concentrate. I don't think it helped that I kept thinking Mother would be home soon and I didn't know what I'd say when she saw Jan there. My earlier bravado had fizzled away.

He didn't stay long. He said his parents would be expecting him.

But we've exchanged phone numbers.

What are they going to think when Jan rings up?

19 JANUARY

Jan still hasn't called. I thought he would this evening. Each time the phone rang I leapt up, sure it was for me. By the time it rang for the fourth time I'd given up. He'd never ring now. Mother picked up the receiver. This time it was for me.

My heart swung like a hammer when I heard her call up the stairs. "It's for you, Katrien."

I walked downstairs as nonchalantly as I could, but I was feeling as if the word JAN was branded on my forehead. In my head I was rehearsing what I'd say. Then I saw Mother smile. That was when I knew it wasn't Jan, and my heart slowed to its normal beat. I took the receiver from her.

"Hello, Katrien," Anneke said.

"Oh, hello, Anneke," I said, trying to hide my disappointment.

I couldn't have managed it very well for she immediately said: "What's wrong?"

"Nothing."

"It sounds as if there is."

I made some excuse and pulled myself together. I haven't told her about Jan. But then what could I tell her? *There's a boy I like, but I haven't heard from him.* The phone has rung three more times since then. That's seven times this evening. Seven times! It *never* rings as often as that. Jan still hasn't phoned. I'm trying not to think he's changed his mind.

20 JANUARY

Pieter is up to something, but I don't know what. He hasn't told me, of course. He was in his room with friends, music playing softly. Suddenly he turned up the volume. It was so loud. I went to his room and opened the door. Everyone looked up – then at each other. Pieter asked what I was doing, barging in like that. I said stiffly I'd like him to remember he wasn't the only person in the house. I must have sounded like Mother! He turned the volume down, but a few minutes later, I heard the door open and the boys' voices as they tramped noisily downstairs. Gone somewhere else to discuss their secret business no doubt. That doesn't sound much, I know, but I'd seen Pieter stuff something under his pillow and his face had looked very furtive. I know that he's got a secret. I wish he'd share it with me. We used to be close and it makes me sad to think that we might be growing apart.

22 JANUARY

At last! Jan has rung. It was a rather odd conversation. It didn't help that Mother was in the hall, waiting for *her* call. At least I managed to grab the receiver before she did. I'd given up expecting him to ring so I felt all calm, and then I heard Jan's voice say, very politely, please may I speak to Katrien.

It was so unexpected that I couldn't think what to say. Everything I'd rehearsed flew straight out of my head.

"Hello?" Jan said when I didn't say anything.

"Sorry," I said quickly. "This is Katrien." Mother was still hovering, waiting for me to finish. I wished she would go. This was a private call, between me and Jan. Then I suddenly had this odd feeling that his mother was probably doing the same at his home. It was a bit of a squash in his flat, he'd told me. Maybe it was hard to have any privacy now? Maybe that was why he hadn't rung before?

"Katrien? Are you still there?"

"Yes, I am. Sorry," I said again. I'd been miles away in my thoughts, the receiver still pressed to my ear.

"Is tomorrow after school all right then?"

He was talking to me but I hadn't taken in what he was saying.

"Sorry... I..."

"I was saying maybe we could meet again, if you like. Same place?"

"That would be nice," I said politely. Mother was still waiting, and she'd be bound to ask who I was talking to, and what would I tell her? *You know that boy called Jan? Well, I bumped into him in the street and last week he came over. I gave him tea and he helped me with my maths homework. Oh, and by the way, he's Jewish. And he wants to see me again.*

Maybe not.

It's mad but after I put the phone down I felt happy. Yes I know that there are all sorts of reasons why we shouldn't be friends. There is hardly anywhere we can go together. On the front of shops, cafés, restaurants, cinemas, theatres, even parks and public libraries there are these big signs bearing the words "Jews not welcome here". Even the beach is out of bounds now! There's hardly anywhere where you're welcome if you're Jewish. I've never really stopped to think what that must be like. After all it's never affected me before. I can go where I like, shop where I like and walk where I like – unless of course there's an air raid on. Jan's world has shrunk until almost all that's left to him is to go for a walk. Even then, it's hard to think where we could go. The river? I'd need to wear my warmest clothes if we went there. It's awfully cold by the river in winter. The wind blows straight through you.

Fortunately Mother didn't ask who'd rung, for the phone rang again as soon as I'd put down the receiver and it was for her, so maybe she forgot. I'm not going to let myself worry about that anyway. I've got other things to think about.

Tomorrow, after school, I'll see Jan again. I can hardly wait!

23 JANUARY

Am sitting on the radiator, my diary balanced on my knees. I have put on so many pairs of socks that I can't pull on my slippers. The radiator is barely tepid but it's better than nothing. Gradually feeling is returning to my frozen body. I pray that spring comes early this year.

I don't think I'll ever forget Jan's face when he saw me today. I told him it wasn't funny and he shouldn't laugh. I knew I looked funny though. I'd seen myself in the mirror when I'd gone into the school toilets to change. I'd so many clothes on that I could hardly do up the buttons on my coat! Fortunately Anneke was going out for supper at a relation's and so I was able to cycle off on my own. I'd brought another jumper too – for Jan. He looks as if he doesn't have enough warm clothes. It's an old one of Pieter's. He never wears it and won't miss it. I knew that wherever we were going it would be cold – and it was. Very. There is nowhere warm we can go – at least, not together. Not until one of us screws up enough courage to tell our parents that we're friends. I don't think either of us feels quite brave enough for that.

We did go to the river. It was even colder than I'd expected. We walked very fast down one bank. Then very fast back again. We saw hardly anyone. You'd need to be mad or desperate to be walking by the river on a day like today. We saw a few seabirds who'd flown upriver and a man repairing a barge gave us a curious look. He must have thought we were quite mad. I don't know what Jan thinks of me, but he must like me a bit, or he wouldn't have put us through this. We couldn't even talk much. The wind blew our words away as soon as they left our mouths. But Jan was very pleased with the jumper. I told him he could keep it for now. His coat's too thin, and I wish he'd throw away that awful scarf. I'll knit him a new one, but I won't tell him. It'll be a surprise.

26 JANUARY

It's still very cold. I'm sitting close to the window – and I can see ice on the inside. Outside, I can hear children shout as they slide down the frozen pavement. It's given me an idea. I can't think why I didn't think of it before. If Jan has got skates, we could go skating on the canal. I don't think there's any law against that. I've begun to knit him a scarf. Knitting is one thing I am good at. And I'm quite a good cook. Mother says if I was less untidy I might make someone a very good wife one day. I'm not sure what I think about that! I have other plans for my future apart from being a good Dutch housewife. I've never talked to Mother about them. She wouldn't understand. She met Father when she was quite young and was happy to settle down. She seems to like being at home and looking after us all. I think it would be dull. I want to see the world – if the War ends before I'm too old.

On Saturday if there are enough clothing coupons left I'll go into town and buy some more wool to finish Jan's scarf. I'm going to knit him some gloves too if there's any wool left over. His have holes in them.

27 JANUARY

Isn't it funny. Jan and I both had the same idea. We both said "let's skate" at the same time. So tomorrow that's what we're going to do!

28 JANUARY

We went skating today. We chose a canal nice and far from both our homes. It was quiet and we didn't see anyone we knew. And we were so well wrapped up no one would have recognized us anyway. Jan took my hand and we skated off together. Soon we were going faster and faster. It felt almost like flying. It wasn't as cold as it had been by the river. All the same I felt quite envious as I looked at people sitting in the little cafés that ringed the canal. The lights had come on inside and they looked so warm and cosy. If only we could have gone in, too. I was longing for a mug of steaming hot chocolate! I didn't say anything to Jan though. I didn't want him to think I minded. And I don't. Not really. I hope he feels the same. I wish I knew.

3 FEBRUARY

Fell asleep in our English lesson this afternoon – my favourite lesson, too! I'd struggled to stay awake all morning. It wasn't just me either. I only woke up when I heard Christiaan snore! It made everyone laugh. Even our teacher. She looked tired, too. It's not easy to sleep in a cellar with your legs resting on the mudguard of your bike! That's where we shelter when there's an air raid. At least we don't have to share it with anyone else. Mother has tried to make it comfortable but it's more cramped than cosy.

As soon as I was in bed, the sirens began to wail. I pulled a jersey on over my dressing gown, grabbed a blanket and my knitting and went downstairs. Sitting there, squinting in the light of the one candle Mother allowed, my needles clacking away helped distract me from what was happening outside. Shells whistled and fell – one sounded so close the whole building shuddered! We all jumped and looked at each other. I knew the same thought was in our minds. *That could have been us.* When it's that close it reminds me of the danger we're in. I send up a prayer. Please, God, don't let it be us.

I had to make do with an oily cushion for a pillow. That was Pieter's fault, he'd oiled his bike in there earlier. Mother had boiled up a tea bag in the kettle for tea, which had to last till the All Clear sounded. Lying there, one ear on Father, who was trying to distract us by telling us stories about his medical student days, another on what was happening outside, I thought how topsy-turvy the world has become. It's our Allies who are dropping the bombs, and our enemies who are firing at them to try and make them stop. Every time I hear the drone of the planes I feel my teeth begin to chatter. I don't want the Nazis to shoot down the planes, but neither do I want my city to be bombed. The Allies are targeting the Nazis' munitions, but they also try to destroy all the things that make our lives still bearable – like the gasworks, and the railway station – and all too often they miss and hit a shop or someone's home. I'd like to feel we're reasonably safe here – there's no factory, power station or railway very close to us. Then I thought about Jan. How safe are he and his family? I don't even know where he lives. I just hope it's not near anything the bombers target.

It's always such a relief when the All Clear sounds and we can climb tiredly back upstairs again. Last year a lot of planes flew over and dropped tea bags all over the country! We all went out to look for them. I didn't find any, but Anneke's cousins in the country did very well!

5 FEBRUARY

I'm lying here, dreaming. I've never met a boy quite like Jan before. He's brave, and clever, and kind. And he has these amazing eyes. I'm trying to think how to describe them. Like the sky on a really lovely summer's day. Blue, a warm blue, like that. I haven't told Mother and Father that we're friends. I think about it, but something holds me back. I don't know what they'd feel about it. They never mention him anyway. It's probably just as well.

I've got Jan's old scarf. He doesn't know that I've got it, but he won't miss it. He left it on the ground when he put my one on. Now we both have something that belongs to the other. I like that.

I wish I knew what he thinks of me. Oh I know he thinks I'm brave, but does he really like me, or am I just someone to spend time with? He's told me he does remember seeing me around at school. I wonder if that's true, or he's just saying it because I told him I remember him. If the Nazis hadn't invaded our country, he'd still be there. Sometimes I dream about what that might have been like, but not often, because it makes me sad. We could have got to know each other, like you do your friends. We could have walked about openly and done all the things my other friends still can. I feel as if we've a lot of catching up to do – to make up for all that missed time. I was only thirteen when the Nazis invaded Holland. He was fifteen.

I'm beginning to realize how important it is to make the most of every moment. I used to think I had all the time in the world. Seize the moment, Father says, and he's right. It's easy to forget, though, so I'm writing it here. Maybe that will help.

I wish we could spend more time together. It always goes so fast. We always meet in the same place. We try and avoid talking about the War. We don't want to spoil our time together. I asked him what he'd planned for us this time. You never know with Jan! When he'd rung he'd said he had a surprise for me. I was longing to know what it was. I spotted the knapsack on his back and he had a rolled-up rug under one arm. We could snuggle under it together. He was grinning broadly. "Where are we going?" I asked.

"It's a surprise," he said.

"You're going to have to tell me."

"No I don't."

"I've got a surprise, too," I said. I held the scarf I'd brought him behind my back. It wasn't the one I'm making – that's not finished yet – but an old one of mine.

"What is it?"

"Tell you if you tell yours."

"Never."

"Then you'll never know," I teased.

Suddenly he lunged at me and tried to grab my arm. I leapt away from him and held the scarf high above my head. "Tell," I said, "or you don't get it."

"I will, but not yet."

"You'll get it when you do," I said.

"I don't want to spoil it."

I admit I didn't want him to do that. I lowered my arm and shoved the scarf at him. "Here you are," I said. "I thought you might find it warmer than yours."

He was holding it and looking at it.

"For me. Really for me?"

"For you."

He gave me one of those lovely smiles. It made me feel a bit shy and I looked away. When I looked back he had taken off his old scarf and wrapped my one round his neck. He left the old one on the ground. I picked it up when he wasn't looking, and stuffed it in my satchel.

"Now follow me." As I've said, Jan has a long stride, but he shortened it again so that I could keep up. I couldn't think where he was taking me. We seemed to be weaving about all over the place. "Where are we going?" I asked again.

Then he said: "Shut your eyes."

"Why?" I asked.

"Just shut them."

I shut them and felt his hand reach for mine. As it slid into my palm, I felt my heart begin to jump about inside. His hand was surprisingly warm and felt nice. I wondered if he'd told me to shut my eyes so he could take my hand? If he'd really wanted to and didn't know how to ask?

He gave my hand a slight tug. "Come on!" Of course he'd only taken it so he could guide me. Katrien, you are silly!

It felt strange walking behind Jan, with my eyes shut. At first I shuffled a bit, afraid that I'd fall, or trip over. Then I began to relax. I couldn't think where he was leading me, but it felt as if we were walking quite a long way – it's hard to be sure when you have your eyes shut. Then he stopped and I nearly walked straight into his back! He told me I could open my eyes.

I opened them slowly, wondering what I'd see. It took a minute to orientate myself and when I did, I gasped. I felt as if I'd been transported to some magical place far away from the city. I was standing on a large square of grass, surrounded by trees. There were gravelled paths, neatly clipped box hedges and flowerbeds – empty of course since it's winter. Even a fountain, though it wasn't playing. It was like what a park might look like if it was in miniature. The frosty grass shone like diamonds. I felt as if I was in fairyland.

"Do you like it?" he said. He was looking at me as if he minded what I thought.

"I do," I breathed. "It's beautiful. Where are we?"

He grinned at me. "About five minutes away from where we met."

I told him I didn't believe him. He said he'd deliberately tried to confuse me, and so we'd walked round and round in circles.

What I really wanted to know was *why* he'd brought me there. I hoped it was because he wanted to be on his own with me.

I didn't say that of course, and all he said was that it was his secret place. And that very few people knew about it. "Isn't it private?" I wanted to ask, but I didn't want to spoil the moment. I gazed up at the sky, at the heavy snow-laden clouds. They looked as if they were about to burst.

He'd even brought tea! It was pretty weak but in that place it was like sipping an elixir. He gave me the cup and he drank straight from the flask. We sat down on the small rug he'd brought, pulling it up around our knees.

I asked him what the garden was like in summer and he told me to shut my eyes again and he described it to me. When he'd finished I had a whole picture in my mind – of what it looked like, season by season, and when we came to winter, I opened them again. I thought how different he was to Pieter, who'd just have listed the names of the flowers. But for Jan, they seem to mean something. He says he comes here a lot, but that I'm the only person that he's brought here. It made me feel special. "It's a secret between us then," I said. "I'll keep it, don't worry." Of course I've confided the secret to my diary. But that doesn't count. Anyway, that's a tiny secret next to the big one which no one at all knows about – our friendship.

He knows a lot of things I don't. I wasn't surprised when he told me he wants to go to university. He said he would be the first in his family to go there. I asked him what he'd study. "Father wants me to be an engineer," he told me. "I thought I'd like to do that, but now I'd rather study history." When I asked him why, he said that he wanted to understand why there were wars. Then he fell silent and I didn't know what to say. What could I say after that? I think everyone should study history, and someone should have made Adolf Hitler study it, too. Then maybe he'd have realized how stupid and pointless wars are, and how people are really all the same underneath.

We'd just finished our tea when snow began to fall. So we made a sort of tent of the rug and crawled underneath. The ground was hard and too cold to sit on. I sat up on my heels and moved closer to him. "Cold?" he said. I nodded. I felt his arm come round me, slowly, almost shyly, as if he was asking if I minded. I leant against him. It felt very romantic, sitting there next to him, his arm round me, watching the snowflakes dance through the air. Jan says we'll come back. I wonder when that will be. Maybe we'll come back next year. Maybe by then the War will have ended.

We couldn't sit like that for long. It was far too cold and the snow was beginning to fall more thickly, weighing down

the blanket we were sheltering under. I got up reluctantly –
sad that we had to leave. I watched while Jan hastily shoved
the flask and cup into the knapsack. We shook out the rug,
but it was too wet and heavy now to fold properly, so I draped
it over the handlebars of my bike. He didn't make me shut my
eyes again. I don't think I would be able to find my way back
there anyway. Snow was falling so thickly it almost blinded us.

Luckily no one saw or heard me come in. I was soaked
through. As I crept across the hall, I could hear the radio
on in the kitchen. I slipped upstairs and dried myself off. I'd
have loved a bath, but the water was cold.

It's dark now but I can just about make out the shapes of
snowflakes whirling against the window. I remember how we
sat under the rug and gazed out at them, and the feel of his
arm round my shoulder. We won't be able to go back there
till the snow has gone. Jan's going to ring me when he's made
another plan for us to meet. Let it be soon!

7 FEBRUARY

I'm writing with my gloves on. It makes it hard to write
neatly, but it's too cold to write without them. I've made a
sort of tunnel of my bedclothes and I'm lying inside it on my

stomach, my diary propped up on the pillow. My books are heaped up next to me and stare at me accusingly. I've hardly made a start on my homework. Mother doesn't understand why I don't go downstairs where it's warmer. But I can't write my diary downstairs. It's private!

Jan and I have had several conversations on the phone. We tell each other about our day. He makes me laugh – the stories he tells. I wonder how many of them are true! Mother said tonight that the phone is for the whole family to use, not just me. I thought she might ask who it was I was speaking to, but she didn't. I haven't asked him what his family thinks, or if they even know about me. Would they mind if they knew I was a Gentile girl? I still feel a bit as if I'm on shifting ground. Are we just friends, or does he like me more than a friend? I haven't known him long. I hardly know him at all, yet I feel as if I do. Maybe it's because of what happened when I met him that I feel close to him. But does he feel the same? I'm scared to ask. I'm scared what he'll say. Maybe he's scared, too?

9 FEBRUARY

Have finished knitting Jan's scarf and have just begun on the gloves. I hope they're the right size! Am knitting as fast as I can, so Jan will be able to wear them before the winter is over. I took my knitting into school with me today and in breaks between lessons I pulled up the lid of my desk to knit in private. Or so I thought. Nearly jumped out of my skin when I saw Saskia's face peering round the desk lid. She asked what I was knitting. "Oh, just some gloves," I said, and shrugged, trying to make it sound as boring as possible. I must have succeeded, for she turned away to talk to someone else.

10 FEBRUARY

Saw Jan today. We just walked together round the quieter streets. Even that felt a bit frightening. We saw a crater where a bomb had landed. Right in the middle of the street. It was a long way from any munitions factory or power supply. Two boys were peering in to see how deep it was. Jan and I just looked at each other. I wondered if he was thinking the same as me. *Please don't let one land on him*. We rarely talk about air raids, but each time the All Clear sounds I wonder if he is safe. I've added him to the list of people I pray for each night.

I wish we could go back to Jan's secret place. But even Jan thinks it's too cold and snowy to go there now. We'll have to find somewhere else. In the summer we're going back to the river. Jan's said he'll teach me to sail. I'm happy that he's making plans for us. But I am going to have to be more careful. Mother has noticing eyes and tonight she said: "You were late home again today. Why?"

Is she timing me?

"Was I?" was all I could manage. As soon as I've cycled back with Anneke I cycle off to meet Jan. It's just as well she turns off before I do.

Mother gave me the look she always gives me when she's disappointed in me. "Try not to be late tomorrow," she said. One of her friends is coming for tea, and Mother says she'd like to see me. I don't believe Mrs Linker would care if she saw me or not. Mother just wants to make sure I'm home early for once.

12 FEBRUARY

Anneke is suspicious and I'm not surprised. Something really embarrassing happened today. I found myself giggling out loud – right in the middle of a lesson. I was miles away, thinking about something Jan had told me on the phone last night. I looked up to find the room had gone quiet and everyone was staring at me. Maarten had a supercilious expression on his face. Anneke had a questioning one on hers. The teacher asked dryly if I would like to share with the class what I'd found so amusing about what he'd been telling us. It was a history lesson. I hadn't a clue what he'd been saying of course, and he knew it. So I just slid down into my seat and muttered that I was sorry. I seem to be apologizing a lot lately. He kept me in and I had to write out fifty times that I would attend in class.

I hoped that Anneke would have gone by the time I finished, but as I cycled up to the gate I saw her waiting for me. I felt uneasy as we cycled off together. She was bound to ask questions – questions I wouldn't be able to answer. But she simply asked me if I'd like to go back with her. I told her I'd need to ask Mother. That she was being very particular about the hours I kept. "You can ring from our house," she protested.

"I don't think I should," I said. I couldn't meet Anneke's eyes and I know she noticed. Jan was going to ring me that evening. We've worked out a good time for him to call, and I wanted to be there when he did.

"I don't feel as if we see each other very much now," she said.

"We cycle home together every day," I reminded her.

"That doesn't count! Anyway, it's not just that. You seem so – so *distant*."

I dropped my eyes. She sounded a bit sad, and I felt guilty.

I haven't been much of a friend to Anneke lately. "I'll ring you when I get home," I said.

"Promise?"

"I promise."

I got home on time and waited for the phone to ring at the appointed hour. It didn't – because it couldn't. Pieter was on the phone for hours! He kept looking round at me and frowning every time I went back to see if he'd finished. By the time he had I knew it would be too late for Jan to ring. And I was right. He didn't.

I've just remembered something. I forgot to phone Anneke! And I gave her my word, too. She'll be so fed up with me.

13 FEBRUARY

I've had to tell Anneke about Jan. I didn't want to, but I had no choice. If I hadn't she'd never have forgiven me. And she's always been a good friend. I didn't want to lose her friendship.

She gave me an ultimatum, which I found on my desk as soon as I sat down in class this morning. I put it on my lap and unfolded it to read while the register was being taken. It was short and to the point. "Explain – or else. A"

I scribbled a hasty answer – "Let's talk at break" – and slipped it on to her desk. I saw her read it, then she nodded, without looking at me.

It was an awful morning. She didn't speak to me once, and, what was worse, she kept leaning across me to talk to Saskia, laughing at what Saskia said as if she was her new best friend. It made me feel miserable to be so pointedly ignored. I felt as if she was saying to me: "See. I have other friends. I don't need you." If I wasn't to lose her friendship I was going to have to be honest with her.

When the classroom emptied at break, we remained at our desks. I was in a quandary. I couldn't think what I'd say to her. I'd meant to tell her one day, when things were clearer between Jan and me, and I had only myself to blame that I was having to now.

As soon as we were alone she swivelled round in her seat. She'd folded her arms and I felt my heart bump up and down uncomfortably: "All right, so what happened? Why did you break your word?"

The coldness in her voice made me flinch. If only she'd not put it so … so *baldly*.

I took a deep breath – and told her. She was silent, her eyes fixed on me as I stumbled through my explanation. I told her everything. Well, nearly everything. Everything I felt I could.

"Oh, Katrien," she said when I'd finished. She gave a little smile, it wavered, but it was better than nothing.

"I wanted to tell you, but…"

"You don't know what he feels yet?" she suggested.

I nodded.

She'd unfolded her arms and I felt myself relax a little.

"I've a suggestion," she said. "Ask him to join us one time. We could go out in a group together."

"I can't do that!" The words burst from me before I could stop them. Anneke looked startled. I felt my cheeks flush. I'd done it now.

"Why ever not? Don't you want him to meet your friends? Maybe you should ask him and see what he says. If he likes you, he'll be pleased."

"Because…" I knew I could trust her, but how could I say that she must never breathe a word to anyone else. If ever Saskia found out, Maarten would. I remembered the expression I'd seen on his face that day outside Mr Breitkopf's shop. *Why should I help him? He's a Jew.* But even if I was wrong about Maarten, there were others … others I didn't even know. That was the trouble. I *didn't* know.

"There's something you haven't told me, isn't there?" A cold tone had crept back into Anneke's voice.

I doodled with my pen while I tried to work out what to say. My hand shook. Didn't she understand how hard this was for me? Why wouldn't she stop asking questions? Why wouldn't she leave me alone?

I looked up.

She was still waiting.

It was no use. I had to tell her. But before I could she said: "He's Jewish." She looked me full in the face.

I nodded. It was easier than speaking.

"Oh, Katrien," she said again. I felt I could see in her eyes that she thought I was mad, so I explained about the day I'd met him. And how brave and nice and funny he was. I must have gone on and on because in the end she said: "Stop! I realize he's perfect."

"Don't joke," I said annoyed.

"Sorry. I didn't mean to. I do understand." But I don't think she does. Not truly.

All she can see is that I like a Jewish boy. And that's typical Katrien. Pick the difficult option. Not that you can't help who you like.

"The War won't go on for ever," I said stubbornly.

She nodded slowly. "So that's why you don't trust Maarten. I think you're wrong about him. He was just afraid. Not many people are brave enough to stand up to them." She gave me a serious look, then reached over and laid her hand on mine. "Don't look so worried. Your secret is safe with me."

"I know it is." I heard my voice wobble.

"Oh, come here, Katrien." She moved her chair close to mine and put her arm round my shoulders and gave them a squeeze.

I told her I was lucky to have her as a friend.

"You are!" she said.

I managed a smile.

Then she said that if it would help, she would cover for us if we ever needed it. I gave her a big hug. I don't deserve such a loyal friend. I really don't.

16 FEBRUARY

Gave Jan the scarf and gloves today. At least I'd managed to finish them before the end of winter. He was so pleased. "Oh Katrien," he kept saying, staring at them as if he couldn't believe it. "For me?"

He said it was the nicest present he'd ever had and pulled on the gloves at once. He promised they fitted him perfectly. I wound the scarf round his neck. His eyes were smiling into mine as I did it and for one wild moment I thought he was going to kiss me but he didn't. I wonder if he ever will? Or have I got it all wrong and he really only likes me as a friend? If only I knew!

4 MARCH

I don't know what to think. I'm such a mixed bag of emotions. One minute I'm cross, then I'm upset, then I'm worried, then I'm cross again. Jan didn't turn up at our meeting place this evening, and I don't know why. He didn't phone to explain and I couldn't phone him either. Mother kept me busy all evening helping her with a pile of mending. I had to try and hide how I felt. It wasn't easy. And she gave me some horrible jobs to do. I had to mend a huge tear in the only pair of trousers Pieter has that aren't too short for him – can't think how he did that, it looked as if he'd been climbing trees – and after that I had to let out the hems on my summer dresses. I wish I could have some new ones, but clothing is rationed, too. I'll feel embarrassed wearing these. They are so girlish. If only Mother understood. It made me feel as if I was being punished for "sending her out of her mind with worry" as she called it. Even though I'd explained about the puncture.

It's nearly dawn now, and I'm sitting near the window so there's just enough light to write by without my torch. I've long ago given up trying to sleep. Maybe writing everything down will help.

This afternoon – after cycling back with Anneke – I'd gone on to meet Jan. It was icy. Even wrapping my arms around myself and marching up and down didn't warm me up at all. My cheeks felt as if they were being scraped by knives. People gave me odd looks. The shadows began to lengthen. I must have looked at my watch about a hundred times. Ten minutes. Eleven. Twelve. How slowly the time passes when you're waiting for someone. Jan didn't come. I felt upset. Then annoyed. If he'd changed his mind couldn't he at least have told me?

After fifteen minutes I gave up. Jan wasn't coming. I'd better go home. I got back on my bike and cycled off as fast as I could. There seemed to be more soldiers than usual on the streets. They stared at me but they didn't try to stop me. Good thing I'm blonde – the Nazis' favourite colour. I was feeling really annoyed with Jan for not turning up – and letting me stand about in the icy cold – and I wasn't looking where I was going and bumped right into a huge pothole. I clung on tightly to the handlebars and somehow I managed not to fall off, but as I was cycling away, I could hear an odd sort of hissing noise coming from the front tyre. I got off to look at the cause, though I hardly needed to. Of course I'd got a puncture. I nearly exploded then!

It would have been worse if I hadn't been able to explain about the puncture. But it was bad enough. Mother said that she'd been phoning all my friends to find out where I was. None of them knew. Anneke would have covered for me, but she had gone out. "So where were you?" she asked. I got a puncture cycling home, I told her. I'd had to walk most of the way. "Ummm," she said, and gave me a most suspicious look. I felt as if the truth was branded on my forehead in HUGE letters!

Pieter's pumped up the tyre and stuck a bit of rubber over the hole. Fortunately, it's not a big one. "You'd better ride slowly," he said. "I don't know how long it will hold. And watch out for those potholes," he added.

Thank you, Piet. I needed reminding. That's a big help.

Writing it down hasn't helped at all. Why did Jan let me down? Couldn't he at least have phoned? Doesn't he know I'm bound to worry? It's awful not knowing. He'd better ring tomorrow – or else.

5 MARCH

Jan has just rung. His aunt came over and he couldn't get away. "I feel bad that I couldn't let you know," he said. "I hated thinking of you waiting and waiting."

He hated thinking of me waiting and waiting. I suppose that's something. Actually I felt happy he'd said that and then I felt I could tell him I was relieved he was all right. At least I think I did. I'm not sure exactly what I said. I'd quite forgotten I'd been angry.

We're going to meet up tomorrow. I didn't tell him about all the soldiers I'd seen on the streets. Should I have? I don't want to. I have this awful feeling there's a time coming when it won't be safe for us to meet at all. We must just make the most of what we have – for as long as we can.

Unless … unless I tell Mother about him? But what if she refuses to let me see him? Why do I think she will? I'm just too afraid to find out. I daren't risk it.

6 MARCH

I am thinking back over the evening. Sometimes I find myself smiling, ridiculously. I feel as if I'm floating, then I feel so unaccountably weary and all I want to do is crawl under the bedclothes and never come out again. I have a lot to think about. All sorts of things – good things, happy things – and other things I'd rather forget.

I'm not making much sense, am I?

I'll go back to when I met Jan earlier today.

We hadn't made any plans, and we wandered aimlessly around the town. I was thinking that I didn't care where I was, I just liked being with him. I wondered if he felt the same. Or if he was bored. Or if he'd say, *Look, Katrien, it's getting too difficult.* And it is. It was hammered into us today just how difficult. But I'll come to that later.

I'd met him straight from school and was pushing my bike. We were so busy talking we didn't realize that we'd wandered into a square filled with German soldiers. They were making everyone stop to check their ID cards. It's the sort of thing the Nazis like to spring on us – to keep us all on our toes. Next to me I felt Jan stiffen. I said it would be all right, but I was frightened, too. I put my hand in my pocket to check I had my ID card and it was there. It's the one thing I make sure never to leave home without. I saw Jan do the same. Then he took his hands out and plunged them back in again. Then he put them in his trouser pockets. Again, they came out empty. I didn't need to see the look of consternation on his face to know that he had forgotten it. I felt quite sick. Now what were we going to do?

"You'd better pretend you're not with me," he said. "It's my problem – not yours."

I shook my head. "We're in this together," I said.

"No," he said. "We're not."

Before I had a chance to argue he walked quickly away from me. I felt despair. How would he ever get away? German soldiers and agents were everywhere.

In front of me a soldier was checking an old woman's

card. There seemed to be some difficulty as he was taking a long time about it, and she was looking more and more frightened. I felt sorry for her but the longer he took the more chance Jan had to slip away. I focused my eyes on her and tried not to think where Jan was now. Then I heard a voice, a harsh German voice: "Hey you! Halt! Halt now!" I looked up but I knew who he was shouting at. The soldier raised his gun. He was going to shoot! And there was nothing I could do! My heart began to race and my hands felt clammy. Jan ducked just in time and the bullet ricocheted uselessly off a wall. It was so near and so loud that my ears actually hurt. I heard a child cry, saw people's startled faces, and then I glimpsed Jan again, racing away from the square, dodging people, ducking and diving.

The soldier hollered to his companions, and I saw them race out of the square after him. Another blast of gunfire ricocheted across the square. They'd shoot him, or catch him, one of them would, be bound to and then … there was a mist in front of my eyes, so I couldn't see properly, and then I felt someone catch my arm and a voice that seemed to come from faraway was telling me to sit down and put my head between my knees. The world was growing darker and darker. I slid to the ground and bent my head over my knees. Slowly the world began to return.

"Better now?" a male voice said in Dutch close by my ear. He had a thick German accent, and I edged away from him as fast as I could. "Let me help you," he said. I glanced up at him, then quickly away. The soldier was looking attentively at me. I'd seen him before, I didn't let myself think where. "Are you all right? You fainted."

"I'm all right," I said.

He reached down a hand. Reluctantly I let him help me up.

"I think you don't remember me, Fräulein. Me – I always remember pretty girls. My name is Kurt." He gave me a broad smile.

How could he think I cared who he was?

Him a Nazi soldier – my enemy. And then I remembered where I'd seen him before. With Jan, the day I met him. Had he seen Jan and me together? Had he seen Jan run from the square? *What if he found out that he was Jewish?*

"Fräulein." The soldier was saying something to me. In the turmoil of my mind I'd hadn't taken it in. I dragged my attention back to him.

"You aren't well enough to go home on your own, Fräulein. Would you allow me to escort you?"

I nearly shouted "No!" I couldn't let a German soldier escort me home. What would people think? "I am all right now, truly – thank you," I said as politely as I could manage. I wished he would go away. I was trying with all my might to hide how frightened I was. Where was Jan? It was a huge effort not to stare down the street where I'd seen him run.

Had he got away, or...? Awful pictures flooded through my mind. Dreadful pictures, tumbling one after the other. A boy, lying on the ground, in a pool of blood, soldiers standing over him. A boy, hands tied behind him, being marched off to Gestapo Headquarters. I wanted to shut them out, but I couldn't. I took some deep breaths to try and calm myself. I didn't want to faint again!

"We are not all thugs, Fräulein," the soldier said coolly as if he'd read my mind. "Your ID card, please." He flicked through it and told me I might go. He smiled at me again and I forced myself to smile back though he made my flesh creep. I picked up my bike and strolled away, trying to look as casual as if I was out for a walk in the park. I turned into the street I'd seen Jan run down. Then, when I was sure the soldiers could no longer see me, I climbed on to my bike and sped down the street, braking at every side street and alley to stare down it, peering at the houses as I cycled past, wondering if anyone had been brave enough to take him in. He could be anywhere by now. If only those awful images would leave my mind. If only I dared call his name. Exhausted, I got off my bike and leaned back against a wall. I was trying with all my might to hold back my tears. But I was tired and frightened and I longed to be at home. My parents would be worrying about me. What would they say when I got home? How would I explain where I had been? I tried to tell myself that Jan had found his way home. But I couldn't bear to leave until I was sure, until I'd investigated every street and every alley. Until I knew what had happened to him. Long shadows crept up the walls. It was growing dark. Where was he? Was he safely at home, or was he already being interrogated by the Gestapo? Or…

But he's seventeen, I thought. Only seventeen! Surely even *They* couldn't be so cruel. I felt tears begin to trickle down my cheeks. I wiped them away with my sleeve. But they fell more and more, and I was too tired and upset and miserable to care.

"Katrien!" I turned my head. It was Jan. Was it? Yes it was. We stared into each other's eyes.

"Katrien," he said again.

I simply ran at him, and he caught me.

"Oh, Jan. Jan. Jan," I said over and over again. My face was smeary with tears and I clung to him, burying my wet face in his shoulder.

"Katrien," he said. "Oh, Katrien." His arms were tight round me and his face was in my hair. I wanted to say, never do that again, never put me through that again, but I simply clung to him. I didn't care who saw; I didn't care what anyone thought. He pulled me back off the street, round the corner into a little side alley, where it was quieter and no one could see us. I lifted my head to see that he was gazing into my eyes. I held his gaze, drinking in the sight of him, and I saw a little questioning look in his eyes – as if to say, *Is this all right?*, and I think I nodded – and then I saw his face come closer and I shut my eyes as I felt his lips on mine. It was the first time he'd kissed me and I'd often wondered what it would be like. It wasn't my first kiss. I'd been lunged at by boys and had to push them off. But I knew this would be quite different. This time I was kissing a boy I really liked. And it was wonderful. His lips felt warm and sweet against mine. Then he was giving me little kisses all over my face, and saying my name to me over and over again. And my heart felt as if it was singing.

I don't know how long we stood like that, arms wrapped round each other, the shadows lengthening and darkening around us. "We'd better go," Jan said at last. He lifted his face and smiled down at me. I felt as if I'd melt in that smile. He kept his arm round me as we walked down the street. We kept stopping and looking at each other, and smiling. I think he said he was sorry for what had happened, but I no longer cared. We'd at last shown what we felt for each other. That was all that mattered to me then. My feet felt as if they'd sprung wings.

When I was able to speak again, I asked him to tell me how he'd managed to escape. "The soldiers pursued me, but I'd had a good start. Even so, I don't know what would have happened if a man hadn't grabbed my arm and pulled me into a house, just after I rounded the corner. The soldiers ran straight past." He sounded sober. Even though the danger was past, I shivered. I'm sure that the same thought was in both our minds. That man had probably saved Jan's life.

"Did he tell you his name?" He said he had and he had his address, too. "Don't lose it," I said.

"I won't – don't worry."

He put his hands on my shoulders and gazed deep into my eyes. I felt as if I was drowning. Had I minded? he said.

"Had I minded what," I said.

"You know, that I ... that you…"

"Why should I?" I said boldly.

"Oh … because…"

Because you're Jewish, I thought. I wondered if that was why he'd never kissed me before. So I leaned across and gave him a little kiss, just so he knew I liked him. Really liked him. He gave me a huge smile.

All too soon we reached the turning where our ways parted and he left me. I watched as he walked quickly away. I don't know how my feet found their way home. I was still in too much of a dream to think of getting on to my bicycle, to even know where I was going or why.

It was almost completely dark by the time I let myself into the house. Luckily Mother was out so I didn't have to explain myself. Tiredly I picked up the phone to speak to Jan, to make sure he was safely home, but a woman answered and I put the receiver down again quickly.

He hasn't phoned and I want to speak to him. Want to hear

his voice on the end of the line so badly. If I think about him really hard maybe he will know and maybe he will think of me. It feels as if he is. He feels as close as if he's standing next to me. When I go to sleep I'll hold the thought of him to me. Maybe then I'll dream about him. Maybe he will dream about me.

8 MARCH

Jan still hasn't rung. After all that's happened between us! I'm trying not to panic. Has he changed his mind? Has what happened made him see how difficult it's going to be for us? I've picked up the phone at least ten times, but each time I put it down again. I know what Anneke would say! Please phone me, Jan. Please!

10 MARCH

At last he's rung! I was on the point of phoning Anneke and asking her what I should do, when it rang. I grabbed the receiver. "Are you alone?" a voice asked me.

It was Jan. It wasn't Anneke. It was Jan.

"Yes," I said. Mother was in the kitchen with Jacinta, our maid, and the radio was on, but even so I found myself whispering.

There was a long pause. I felt sick with fear as I waited for him to tell me it was over. Then he said: "I've missed you." And all the fear I'd been feeling rolled away like a cloud, and again I had that strange feeling I was floating. I was so happy. He missed me. He'd even told me so.

"I miss you too," I said softly.

I didn't tell him I'd been half out of my mind with worry, or about my other fears.

Then he said he wanted to see me. I felt my heart bump about inside me. I'd been so afraid he wouldn't. Afraid that just as we were getting close he'd tell me he couldn't see me any more.

I am trying not to smile all the time, but smiles keep breaking out on my face in spite of myself. Mother says she's pleased to see me cheerful again. "I've been rather worried about you," she told me. She gave me a searching look as if trying to find out what's caused this dramatic change in my mood. Managed not to blush. At least she hasn't asked any questions.

2 APRIL

Jan's going to take me to meet his family. You'd think I'd feel pleased that a boy I liked wanted me to meet his family. It's a sign he's taking our relationship seriously. I like to think so, anyway. I just wish it wasn't like this. They've been asking questions, he explained. *"Where do you go? Who do you see?"* He hasn't told them what happened in the square, but they worry when he's late. He gave a half smile and hugged his knees. We were sitting side by side in our secret garden. Soon small shoots will spring up in the flowerbeds and it won't be just our secret any more.

I sat there quietly, thinking about what Jan had said. He seemed to understand how I felt. "She'll understand why I like you when she meets you," he said, and he slipped his arm around me. I noticed how he'd said "she". And it's meeting Jan's mother I dread most. I leant back against his shoulder, and felt his arm tighten around me. Then we talked quietly to each other, about our dreams, our hopes and fears. Jan has so many plans for his future. It's the first time I've talked to a boy like this. I've never felt close enough to one before. "Promise me something," I said when we stood up to go.

"Anything."

"You don't know what I'm going to ask yet," I said.

He gave me that smile and I had to concentrate hard before saying: "If anything happens, anything, if we can't see each other. Will you come back for me? When it's all over?"

"Do you even need to ask?" he said softly, his eyes seeking mine.

I felt my heart turn over and over.

I met his gaze and held it. I stared deep into his eyes and I could see the promise written there. It has made me so happy.

5 APRIL

I've just returned from tea with Jan's family. When Mother asked where I was going I pretended I was having tea with Anneke. It was the first thought that came into my head. Afterwards I felt ashamed of myself for not telling her the truth, but I couldn't think what to say. I know I will have to tell her about Jan soon. He will have to meet my parents one day – and now I've met his that day is coming closer. I am dreading that.

I should heed our minister's words. *It's always better to tell the truth.* That morning we'd gone to church as usual.

I'd sat and squirmed on my pew all through the sermon. "Nothing lasting or good can ever be built on lies and deceit," he declaimed. I know he didn't have me in mind, but he seemed to be speaking directly to me. It made me feel very uncomfortable.

As I cycled off to meet Jan I was still feeling uncomfortable – and so nervous. He met me outside his house and unlocked the outer door. I felt even more nervous as we climbed the stairs to the flat. It was then I realized how little I really knew about Jan's family. Jan and I don't talk about our families much.

Now I was going to find out, and I wasn't sure I wanted to. And then it was as if Jan knew how I felt because he took my hand and held it. It felt damp, like mine, so I knew he must be nervous, too. He tried to reassure me. "They'll like you – don't worry," he whispered. His mother opened the door. Jan was still holding my hand. She saw. And I knew at once that she didn't like it. I suddenly remembered how my mother had looked at Jan. Jan's mother was looking at me a lot like that now. It made me feel as if I'd grown a pair of horns.

She stood back to let me walk past her. I know she only did it to get a proper look at me. Her eyes are blue like Jan's but a much colder blue, more like the blue of a winter sea than a summer sky. It was easier when his father came in and Jan said: "Father, this is the girl who rescued me from the police." He thought that was terribly funny at first but then he shook his head and said he didn't know why he was laughing and I must never do that again. It had been a dangerous thing to do and how we'd both been lucky that the consequences hadn't been a lot worse. His mother barely smiled. I'm sure she blames me for it. His younger sister, Ilse, asked if I was going to marry Jan! Her mother told her to be quiet. If I hadn't already felt she didn't like me being Jan's friend I'd have known then. I glanced at Jan. He was blushing. His mother saw, of course. She didn't like that either. Not one bit.

Jan says she will like me when she gets to know me. I wish I could believe it! He told me she is only partly Jewish, but what's happened in the country since the German Occupation has made her more Jewish than the rest of them. He asked if I could understand that. I said I could. She'd rather Jan had a Jewish girlfriend. I kept that thought to myself though. I just hope I can change her mind.

Now comes the part that I like best. After we'd had the fastest cup of tea in history, Jan escorted me downstairs. He wanted to walk me home but I wouldn't let him. "Then I'll say goodbye here," he said, when he'd given up trying to persuade me. "At least there's one good thing about it," he added.

"What's that?" I said.

"It's private." He gave me a long look. Then he took my hand and slowly drew me to him. He kissed me again – a really long kiss this time. We stood there together, holding each other close, until we heard the sound of a key in the lock and jumped apart. But we were still smiling at each other, our eyes on each other's. It was hard to look away. And just as hard to hold his gaze. And isn't it strange how when you like someone your lips can say one thing, your eyes another? The eyes cannot lie. There's a saying I've heard of – that the eyes are the window to the soul. But today I discovered something else. It's through the eyes we can see into another's heart. I feel as if I can see into Jan's heart. And I like what I see.

Now I've got to introduce Jan to my parents. However much I dread it, I know I've got to now. It'd be a lot worse if they found out about him before I tell them. But I can't get rid of the feeling that my mother isn't going to like it any more than his mother does.

17 APRIL

What would I do without my diary! I can write anything in it – anything at all. No one will ever know. Had an awful row with Mother earlier – about Jan. I'd screwed up my courage to tell her, but it was a lot harder than I'd expected – and I'd known it wouldn't be easy. But why did she have to twist things? I'd told her, hadn't I?

If only Father had been home. But he'd rung to say he

didn't know when he'd be back. I couldn't put it off any longer. I'd told Jan I'd phone him later in the evening once I'd spoken to them – to make myself do it. It was the only way. But if Father had been there it might not have gone so wrong. Now Mother will tell him some version of what I told her, twisting the truth in her own special way.

She says I should have told her "*what was going on*" long before now. Then, *how long has this been going on?* And: *if he was a nice boy, don't you think he'd have insisted on coming to meet us?*

And that was before I'd even got round to telling her he was Jewish!

What was I supposed to say to that? *He felt you would be annoyed he hadn't told you when I first brought him here.*

Or: *I knew you'd make things difficult for us.*

Both were true.

Then our conversation – if you could call it that – went something like this:

Me: *You've just said what I thought you would.*

Mother: *So instead of telling us you decided to meet behind our backs?*

Me: *It isn't like that.*

Mother: *So what is it like?*

Me: *What's the point of trying to explain? You won't listen.*

Mother: *Don't talk to me like that.*

She *always* says that when she can't think what else to

say. It's her line of last defence. I felt as if I was under cross-fire and the only reason it stopped was because she'd run out of ammunition. It ended by her saying she was very disappointed in me and sending me to my room, as if I was a child, then she threw in that she'd "talk" to Father.

I know what that means, of course. She will tell him to forbid us to see each other.

I'd told Jan I'd ring as soon as I'd talked to my parents. Now what is he going to think? The phone isn't going to be ringing in his home any time soon. I grow hot and cold thinking that Jan will grow impatient and ring up and that Mother will refuse to let him speak to me. I can just imagine what she'd say: *"I don't want you to see or speak to my daughter ever again."* I'd never hear from him again. I know she's worried that he's Jewish. Now is not a good time to have a Jewish boyfriend, but she says she's much more worried that we'd withheld the truth from her! I've almost lost count of the number of times I've crept out of my room on to the landing, waiting for Father to return. I sit there, shivering, wondering if I dare creep downstairs. The hall is usually empty and the silent phone stares at me invitingly but I simply can't go down. I just know that Mother has her ear pressed to the living room keyhole and will come storming out as soon as I pick up the receiver.

Later: I have the dearest father in the world! He's persuaded Mother to let Jan come over to meet them. He didn't put it like that, of course. But she'd never have agreed otherwise. By then I'd felt as if I'd learned what purgatory was truly like. There were just the three of us at supper – Mother, Pieter and me. (I was allowed downstairs for that.) It was awful. We ate almost completely in silence. I picked at my food – my appetite had quite gone. I don't think Pieter noticed anything. He seems to be in a world of his own these days.

I escaped upstairs as soon as Mother let me. I tried to concentrate on my homework but it was hopeless – the words I was staring at might as well have been in a foreign language for all the sense they were making. All I could think about was that soon Father would be home and Mother would have a serious talk with him. I planned to run downstairs and talk to him before Mother could. In the end I didn't hear Father come in but I did hear his voice. Then I heard Mother say: "Is that you, Klaas?" Too late.

I got into bed and pretended to be asleep. All too soon I heard someone coming upstairs. Father. The door to my room was slightly open. I heard it creak as he pushed it open a little more. "Are you awake, Katrien?" he asked. He didn't sound angry or disappointed like Mother, so I murmured "Yes" and sat up in bed. I felt it sag as he came to sit on it next to me.

In the dark I couldn't see his face very well, but I could tell how he felt from his voice. He said a great many things to me, about being honest and about trust, and being responsible, so it was a good thing he couldn't see mine. He said he wouldn't pretend he'd rather Jan wasn't Jewish since it made everything so much more difficult. But finally he said he'd like to meet that brave boy again, and that Mother would like to, too. I think it would be more accurate to say that he'd *persuaded* her to meet Jan. I wonder how he managed it? I'm quite sure she doesn't want to!

30 APRIL

Jan's coming to tea on Sunday. In three days' time. I've just rung and told him. I feel both terribly nervous and really excited. I wonder if he feels the same? I wonder what he'll tell his parents? I think he was really surprised that Mother and Father agreed. At least he was silent for a time after I told him. I was determined to phone him before he rang me. He must have been wondering why he hadn't heard from me before.

I just wish I could get rid of the nagging feeling that there's something on his mind – something to do with me and him. When I talked to Anneke I tried to explain how it wasn't because of anything he'd said; I just knew. Like you do, sometimes. Anneke says that's my woman's intuition but she also says it is a good sign he's agreed to come. I keep telling myself that she is right, but it's no use. I still have that nagging feeling inside me.

3 MAY

I am so miserable. Jan didn't come to tea. He didn't even let us know! How could he? I felt such an idiot sitting there, at the laden tea table. I'd even made a cake, and Mother had cut up sandwiches. We used up our last egg, too! I'd felt so nervous all day. It had both dragged and raced past.

In the end we began without him. Pieter said he was starving and couldn't sit looking at all that food for a moment longer. Mother said we would wait just another five minutes. They were the longest five minutes of my life. Then I said I would phone and left the room. I had to get out – I was almost in tears. Mother hadn't said so, but I felt sure that she was thinking: *There, I told you so. A nice boy would have kept his word.* I told myself she was wrong. There had to be a good reason why he hadn't come or let us know, though just then I couldn't think of any.

I picked up the phone and dialled Jan's number. It rang

and rang. No one answered. That made me feel still more awful. Thanks, Jan. My humiliation was complete.

Father and I had a talk later. He said there would probably be some very good reason why Jan hadn't come and no doubt I would find out soon. But I could tell from the tone of his voice that he was disappointed in him, too. I longed to climb on to his knee like I used to when I was a child so he could comfort me. But I just nodded and quietly left the room. If Jan doesn't phone me this evening, I never want to speak to him again. Can't write more. Too upset.

Later: Jan did explain – after a fashion. He wrote a note, though I still can't understand why he didn't simply ring. I only got it when Pieter remembered to tell me about it. At night! He was sauntering out of the bathroom when he said, "Oh, by the way, Katrien, I've got a note for you." He said he'd found it pushed under the door – early this morning. Pieter's idea of early morning is about midday. I was really annoyed. All that time Pieter had that note, and didn't even think to tell me. He says he has a lot on his mind and I shouldn't make such a fuss! And anyway how was he to have known who it was from. I told Pieter that I had hoped he'd apologize! I ran downstairs and told Mother but she simply nodded. She didn't say anything about arranging another time and I'm not sure I want her to now anyway.

I don't understand it. Why did he feel able to come to the house to deliver the note, but not come in to tea? And there is something about the note that bothers me. After asking me to apologize for him to my parents, he asks me to meet him, at our usual place, near the church by the entrance to the Jewish Quarter – in three days' time after school.

"You will understand when you see me," he wrote. That's all the explanation I've got! Has he been set on by Nazi thugs again? Is he ill? If only I knew. He signed it simply "Jan". No kisses. Nothing. I don't know what I was expecting, but it was a bit more than that!

4 MAY

The term has barely begun and already I'm longing for it to be over. Then there won't be so many people I'll have to pretend in front of. And I won't have to see Maarten's horrible sneering face – but I shouldn't waste precious paper writing about *him*.

The girls and boys in my class make me mad. They chatter away, behaving as if nothing has changed. I suppose it hasn't – for them. I feel as if I've aged around 100 years these past few months. They seem so … so *young*. Even Anneke irritated me today. I knew she was longing to hear all about the tea. But couldn't she tell how I felt?

I did confide in her later though. I couldn't avoid it for ever. She said she'd wanted to phone but hadn't liked to. And then in class today … and she pulled a face. I almost felt myself smile. It isn't Anneke's fault I'm upset with Jan and I shouldn't take it out on her. She is a good and loyal friend. She was indignant when I told her he hadn't come! Then when I explained that Pieter had picked up Jan's note but had forgotten to give it to me, she said: "Well, that's boys for you!"

I did manage a smile then. She says I mustn't worry, that he will have had a good reason for staying away, and that at least he still wants to see me. It's *why* he wants to see me that worries me though. If he doesn't want to meet my family, what does that mean for us? I could see that she was puzzled, too, though she didn't say so.

Must stop now. Mother's calling. I've got to paste a cheerful face on to mine at least until I'm back in my room again.

5 MAY

What *is* Pieter up to? He slipped out of the window – *my* window! – when I was downstairs. He didn't tell me where he'd been and he still hasn't. He'd waited till we'd had supper before escaping. I suppose he reckoned he'd be back before anyone noticed.

It was a while before I realized he'd gone. I was in the kitchen helping Mother wash the dishes.

Then I went upstairs to fetch my books. Father had said he would help me with my maths homework. The window was open and I went to close it. As I pulled it down I nearly had the shock of my life! Someone was crouching on the balcony below! I nearly screamed – then I saw who it was. My idiot brother! He put a finger to his lip and indicated that I should pull up the frame for him. I pulled it up hard and stuck my head out. "What are you doing out there?" I hissed. He didn't answer, just reached up with his hands to grab the sill and haul himself in.

"Thanks, Sis," he said.

"Where have you been?" I asked.

"Don't ask," he said shortly.

"You must tell me, Piet, or I'll have to tell Mother and Father."

"Whatever you do, don't do that."

"Why not?"

"Look, believe me, it's better you don't know," he said, which was hardly reassuring. He had his knapsack on his back. It looked bulky.

"What's in that?" I asked suspiciously.

"Just university stuff," he said.

Did he really expect me to believe that?

"Open it!" I demanded.

"Don't be ridiculous, Katrien!"

"Show me!"

He looked at me as if I was off my head.

"I'm waiting," I said. "If you don't tell me, I'll go downstairs right now…"

I marched to the door. I'd meant what I'd said.

"Oh very well." He opened the knapsack and tipped the contents on to the bed.

Out fell two or three books and some paper and pens. I picked up one of the sheets of paper. It had lots of calculations on it. Pieter is good at maths. I put it down. The figures meant nothing to me.

I was silent as he stuffed everything back into his knapsack. I didn't say I was sorry. I wasn't. There had to be a reason why he felt the need to creep in through my bedroom window rather than enter by the front door like a normal person. But would he tell me? No!

6 MAY

"So now you know," he said. He'd covered it up – that hateful yellow star – as soon as he'd shown me. In the middle was one single word in black. *Jood*.

"I hate it," he said. "I'd tear it off if I could. But they'd never let me."

"So that's why you didn't come?" I said. "It doesn't make any difference to me." I was so relieved he hadn't said he didn't want to see me any more that I forgot to be cross. He'd explained why he hadn't phoned – there had been a problem with their line, which was why it simply rang and rang. I hadn't thought of that.

"I thought it might make things worse. Seeing it..." He looked down at the star in disgust.

"I'm sure they know about it." Even I had begun to notice people walking around, yellow stars sewn on their coats and jackets. I'd try not to stare but one woman had caught my eye and immediately crossed her arms over her chest. Like Jan was doing now.

"No, you don't understand. It's as if..." He kicked at a stone. But I did. It was a barrier. The Nazis were deliberately building a wall between us to separate us, one from the other. Brick by brick. Jew from Gentile. Gentile from Jew.

"I won't let them keep us apart," I said. Only you can do that, I added to myself.

He smiled at me, and it was such a sweet smile that my heart missed a beat.

If we hadn't been in the middle of the square, people passing back and forth, I'd have put my arms round him. So far as I knew there was no law against us hugging. Yet.

He moved a bit closer to me and reached for my hand. He held it in his while we gazed at each other.

"We'll have to be even more careful now," he said.

"We will," I said.

We smiled at each other. It was a warm but grey day, but I felt as if I could see a chink of sunshine through the gloom.

We won't let them win.

Now, back home, I'm trying to think where we can meet. It needs to be somewhere private, somewhere we can be sure no one will come. Even our secret garden isn't secret any more – now that it's nearly summer.

10 MAY

I've thought where we can meet. It's brilliant! Why did I never think of it before? The churchyard. The minister won't mind, if he sees us – if he isn't arrested first. His last sermon was a barely coded attack on the Nazis' treatment of the Jews.

This one was a bit different. He talked about the church being a sanctuary – for *everyone*. I'd not been concentrating much up till then but those words made me sit up.

After the service, we lingered in the churchyard, talking to our friends and neighbours. Nice Mrs Meier was there. She was talking to Mother, but I saw her looking thoughtfully at me while I wandered around the yard, pretending to admire the flowers. I wondered briefly if they were talking about me and if Mother had told her about me and Jan, but I was thinking about the minister's words. *The church is a sanctuary.* A few people were laying wreaths on tombstones but most of the time it is a quiet and peaceful oasis where no one comes. Surely we could go there, too? No one would suspect that either of us was Jewish. And if the minister did he wouldn't mind I felt sure. Just so long as Jan didn't...

I rushed home ahead of Mother and Father and immediately dialled Jan's number. I was longing to tell him I'd found a solution to our problem. But when I heard his mother's voice at the other end I was so unnerved that I dropped the receiver on to its cradle. I'll try again tomorrow.

12 MAY

I just hope I've done the right thing. Pieter has joined the Resistance – and has enlisted my help. I know he only told me because he needs it. He's been using my window to climb in and out. I found out an hour ago, when he woke us all up. Honestly, I was petrified. When the doorbell rang I thought it was the police or the Gestapo. It went on so long it sounded like someone was leaning on it. Then it stopped for a minute and I heard Mother say to Father, *Don't you think you'd better get up before they break the door down,* then Father muttering as he went downstairs. I held my breath – then it began. Shouting. A lot of it. I thought Father had gone quite mad. You don't shout at the police. I wanted to crawl under the bed, but I was too scared. Jan says I am brave, but I didn't feel at all brave just then. Then amongst the shouting I heard a voice I recognized –

Pieter's. I'd thought he was in his room! I could still hear his radio playing softly through the wall.

Of course then all my fear vanished. I felt enormously relieved – but angry too. He'd given us quite a fright. And I wanted to know why. Where had he been? What had he been doing?

I waited till everything was quiet again, then I got out of bed and felt my way across the room in the dark, banging my knee painfully on a chair by the door.

I could hear the radio crackling as I opened the door to Pieter's room. My eyes had grown used to the dark now and I could see my brother sitting on the bed, bending over the controls. He jumped as if I was a Nazi stormtrooper, and immediately switched it off. I hobbled over to him.

"Where've you been?" I demanded.

He put a finger to his lip. "Shh."

"It's a bit late for that!" I complained. "You woke us all up! Where were you?"

He shifted up for me, and I sat down next to him.

He hesitated. "I wasn't going to tell you, but you might be able to help."

"How?" I said uncertainly.

"I might need an alibi. I might need you to leave a window open."

Light was dawning slowly. "So you climbed out of my window..."

"…which you then shut…"

"Just like the other day," I finished for him.

He nodded.

I nearly erupted.

"Honestly, Piet. If you want me to help you, you've got to tell me what this is all about."

"I can't tell you every little thing," he said irritably. "Don't you understand? It's not safe to. Awful things are happening." Anger raised his voice. "I can't just sit and do nothing. We've got to resist them. The strike last year failed, so we're doing other things now."

"We?"

He was silent. "Piet, are you … have you…?" I wanted to ask if he'd joined the Resistance. We all know about the Resistance though we are careful not to talk openly about it. A bomb blows up some railway track, or telephone wires are cut. You can't always be sure if it's an Allied bomb or the work of the Resistance.

"If you're asking if I'm working for the Resistance, yes I am."

"Oh Piet, that's so dangerous!" I exclaimed, forgetting to whisper. "You know what happens if you're caught." I moved closer to him.

"Everything is dangerous now – especially if you're Jewish."

I felt as if a cold hand was squeezing my chest.

"What do you mean?" I whispered.

"They won't stop now. It's too easy for them." He was talking almost as if I wasn't there.

"Piet, don't!" I felt my voice wobble.

Piet took my hand and squeezed it. "Don't you worry. I'll take care."

"It's not just *you*…"

"It's that boy you like, isn't it?"

I nodded. What was the use of denying it?

"You're worried that he might be in danger. Don't you worry, we'll think of something."

I'm proud of Pieter, but afraid for him, too. Was I right to agree to help him? Or will I simply make things worse – for all of us? It's a big secret I've been trusted with, and one I'd give anything not to have. But I've sworn to keep it, and I've got to keep my word. And anyway his safety – *all* our safety – depends on it.

13 MAY

I've just returned from delivering a note to Jan. I was lucky. I'd just climbed off my bike when someone opened the outer door and I was able to slip in behind them. My legs were wobbling like jelly as I walked up the stairs. Pushed the note under the door. I had to really push it, too – it got stuck halfway on the mat. As I wiggled it back and forth to ease it further in, I was praying his mother wasn't on the other side, watching. He'll never get it if she finds it first. Then I raced back downstairs before anyone saw me and let myself out. I'll know he's got it, if he comes.

14 MAY

On a warm day the churchyard is a pleasant place to sit. That's all we did, at first. Sit politely side by side, saying little. I don't know what Jan thought but I had a peculiar feeling that God was watching!

After a time we tiptoed over to a tree and hid behind it. There, for the first time in ages, I felt Jan's arms around me again. "Do you think he'll mind?" I said, my voice half muffled against his chest.

"Who – your minister?" said Jan, his arms still round me. I laughed and gazed upwards through the trees at the sky. Little green leaves were uncurling on their branches. It would be summer soon. "No, him," I said. "God."

"If there is a God," Jan muttered. I admit it's getting harder and harder to believe in God, but I put a finger to his lips.

"Don't talk like that!"

He mumbled that he couldn't help it, but I said that at least His representative had made it possible for us to meet even if he didn't know it.

I was so relieved to see Jan. I'd half expected I wouldn't. He told me Ilse had found the note and had given it to him straight away. We've decided now that we'll arrange each meeting at the end of the last one. If either of us is more than ten minutes late the other will know they aren't coming. I feel it is safer this way. It's best that no one knows about us meeting. That's what I said anyway. But I have another reason – I just don't like phoning Jan's house now. Nearly always it's his mother who answers. It's as if she's standing guard over it. And I know what she feels about me seeing her son.

Just like I know what my mother feels about Jan.

We can't come here tomorrow. Mrs Meier has invited us round for tea. I'd rather not go, but she's bound to have made those delicious biscuits. I'll try and see if I can smuggle some out for Jan. He's looking thinner. I don't think he gets enough to eat.

30 MAY

I can't seem to escape that awful yellow star. It's everywhere. I only have to walk down to the end of the road to learn who in my neighbourhood is Jewish. I never used to think about it before.

Earlier today I went out to collect something for Mother from one of our neighbours. On my way back, I ran into one of her friends, laden down with two big bags. They looked awfully heavy so I offered to help her carry them. She looked so embarrassed and said that I was a kind girl, but I'd better not. I felt so mad that she felt like that that when I walked past a soldier afterwards I wanted to shout at him. Anyway I told her I'd tell Mother I'd seen her and I was sure she'd want to pop over later. Mrs Abrahams was nearly in tears. I feel so angry. I hate the Nazis for humiliating my countrypeople – because that is what they are – whether the Nazis understand that or not.

I marched into the house and dumped the package down on the table. Mother saw at once that I was upset and asked me what was the matter, so I told her what had happened. Then she went on and on to Father about how dreadful it was, and how difficult it must be if you were Jewish. I had to leave the room. Couldn't they understand how I felt?

Father had a word with me later. We sat down together and he smiled at me, then he asked how that "nice boy" was. He said he hoped I'd tell him he'd always be welcome in our house. No matter what. I felt too choked up to speak, so I merely hugged him without saying anything. I'm lucky that I have such a kind father. Then I thought about Mother. I don't feel so lucky there. I said I wasn't sure she felt the same. Father says she is just trying to protect me. "You may not realize it, but she does understand." He gave me a kiss.

I've been thinking about what Father said. Jan would be welcome, *no matter what*. It's those last few words I cling to. Should anything awful happen, Jan has a safe haven here. I just hope he'll never need it.

10 JUNE

It's strange. When I'm with Jan I feel so alive. It's as if my other life, my ordinary everyday life, is the shadow life and my real life is the time I spend with him. I could never tell anyone that. I can only write it here. I can write anything in my diary. I wonder I never kept one before.

11 JUNE

I've just read over what I wrote yesterday. Katrien, you're dreaming. Wake up! You're living in a country occupied by a deadly enemy. Awful things are happening all around you. That's reality. It's about time you realized it.

I hated feeling helpless. I found myself wishing there was something I could do – beyond opening windows for Pieter to climb in and out of. I talked with Anneke about it. Father taught me that we should resist tyranny, I told her. But how? She said she felt the same as me.

Unlike me, however, she's had an idea. She told me she'd heard that a number of pupils at another school wear yellow stars, like the ones the Jews are forced to wear. They're not Jewish. They're doing it to show support for their Jewish friends.

"We could do that," I said eagerly.

"We've seen enough stars to make them look right," Anneke said.

"We could cut up some material, make them ourselves."

"Or you could," said Anneke. Anneke is as hopeless at sewing as I am at sums!

We've made a plan now. I'm going to make a sample star and take it into school. Anneke thinks the class would be behind us.

"Or most of it," I said. "What about Maarten?"

"You're wrong about him," said Anneke. "I know you are."

"Give me the evidence and then I'll believe you," I said. I still have doubts about Maarten.

My heart felt a lot lighter as I cycled home. It could be the start of something big. We'd show the grown-ups! There are peaceful ways to demonstrate our disapproval of the Nazis and what they're doing.

It made me feel a whole lot better.

Later: I've had to abandon my plan. Pieter says it's crazy. "Do you want to be put in prison?" he demanded. Apparently that was the fate of those students. So *he* says.

"Don't you know anything?" he sighed. "Take it from me, resisting this lot isn't that easy." I didn't like his lordly tone.

He then went on to tell me something else I didn't know. If you're a Jew and are caught not wearing the star the penalties are much worse. A huge fine and SIX MONTHS in prison!

I can't think where Pieter gets all his information from.

It's awful having to stand by while dreadful things are done – I feel quite helpless. But he says he's sure there will be something I can do – in time. I've just got to be patient. And that he will let me know. But he sounded so patronizing so I don't know if I believe him. But why shouldn't I be involved, too. I'm old enough, aren't I? I'll be sixteen next month!

30 JUNE

It's usually me who gets to our sanctuary first. That's how I think of the churchyard now. Our sanctuary. But for how much longer?

Jan got there before me today, but I didn't know he was there until I saw his head peer round our tree to see who it was.

He looked so relieved when he saw it was me. But even after he'd crept out to sit beside me, I could tell that he was still nervous. He kept looking round and he jumped every time something rustled or stirred.

"What's the matter?" I asked him. "Why were you hiding from me?" I was trying to joke, but his nervousness was beginning to infect me too now.

He took a deep breath. "It's like this," he said. And he told me. It's awful. The Nazis have brought in a whole heap of new decrees to make Jewish people's lives even more difficult. He counted them out on his fingers. First, you can only shop at certain times of the day. Then you cannot use public transport, without first getting special permission. You can't even ride a bike! (Not that Jan has one, of course.) And you have to be home by eight, and then you cannot leave the house again till the next morning. But he was saving the best to last. "I'm not allowed to go into a Gentile's house."

It was a beautiful summer's day, but when he said that I felt as if a huge Nazi hand had reached up and swiped the sun away.

I struggled to find the right words. I couldn't think of any. I told myself that whatever our enemies decreed we'd find a way to be together. Somehow.

I looked into his face. It was as bleak as I felt.

"So you see I can't stay here long," he said. He tried to smile. I felt a moment's panic. Was he saying farewell? Was this the last time I'd sit with him by my side until the Allies had managed to defeat the Nazis? I couldn't even think when that would be. Not for years maybe. I laid my hand on his. If he takes mine and holds it, I thought, we're meant to be together. If not… His fingers curled into mine. It gave me courage to say what I wanted to say. "Jan, they said nothing about meeting Gentiles *outside* their homes. Besides, we've never been bothered here yet."

He turned to smile at me. "Do you remember what I said to you? Soon after I first met you?"

I shook my head. So he reminded me. "I said you

were brave, resourceful and determined. And I was right. You are."

If I am, it's because of you, I thought. But I didn't say it.

He released my hand and jumped down from the wall. "Come on," he said.

"Where?"

"Surely I don't need to tell you." He was smiling into my eyes. Blue eyes, as blue as the summer's sky over our heads. Blue eyes you could drown in.

We stood behind the tree and he took me in his arms. And kissed me. Again and again. He'd never kissed me like that before. I could feel his heart beating rapidly against mine. At last he released me. I was breathless and stumbled slightly and he had to put out an arm to catch me. I leaned against him while he stroked a strand of hair off my face. "I'm going to have to go," he murmured.

He didn't have to tell me why. I knew. He didn't dare miss the curfew. I felt hatred of the Nazis rise in me until I thought I'd choke. How dare they order how we live our lives!

"Here, tomorrow, same time?" he asked.

Not even a regiment of Nazis would keep me away. Our moments together are precious, and I'm determined to make the most of them.

"I'll see you then." I held on to his hand tightly. Gently he released my fingers, one by one. It was so hard letting go.

15 JULY

As soon as I saw Jan today I knew something was the matter. I settled myself down next to him and took his hand. It lay in mine limply, as if he'd rather I hadn't, but didn't like to take it away. I chatted away, pretending I hadn't noticed, but I could tell he wasn't really listening, and I felt really scared. I had to be brave. I had to ask. "Jan, can't you tell me what's wrong?" I said at last.

He withdrew his hand from mine and crossed his arms. He wasn't looking at me when he said: "One of my friends has had call-up papers."

"Call-up papers?" I didn't understand.

He was staring straight ahead. "To work in Germany." He turned his face to mine. It was sombre. "I didn't want to tell you. I didn't want to worry you."

Because you might be called up soon, too.

I felt as if I'd been punched in the stomach. I'd feared something like this would happen. All the restrictions that have been piling up on the Jews. It *had* to mean something.

I knew about the work camps. They were fearful places.

My heart began to beat rapidly. I seized Jan's hand and clung to it, while I thought.

"Jan, we must find you somewhere to hide."

He gave a harsh laugh. I'd never heard him laugh like that before.

"Where will I hide? Besides, there's my family. If I'm called up and don't report, it will be bad for them."

I was silent. I couldn't deny it. "We'll think of something," I said stoutly. Father had said that Jan would always be welcome in our house, but I don't think he's expecting a guest on the run from the Nazis. And Mother. I know she is grieved about the Jews' situation but that's not the same as sheltering a Jewish boy she hardly knows. And Father's made it quite plain that Mother will always put her family first. And as Jan said, there was his family to consider.

I'm not sure what to do, but I must do something. If only I could think *what*.

16 JULY

Just picked up my pen to write. If only I hadn't seen what I did this afternoon. If only it was merely a bad dream. All those people waiting so patiently – for what? Bags and cases heaped around them as if they were going on holiday, and many of the children clutching toys in their arms. Some silent, others chatting. It felt like half of Amsterdam was on the move. Soldiers were everywhere, beckoning people along. "Move! Move!" The people picked up their bags obediently and began to form into a line, as if they had no choice. I longed to tell them to resist. There were enough of them to overcome the soldiers. I heard a child wail and a nervous female voice telling it not to cry, it would be all right. They were going to a nice place. Did she really believe that? I remembered Jan telling me that his friend had been called up. But these were whole families. Why were whole families being sent away? "They're Jews," a man said when I asked – though that was obvious enough – by now everyone in the country must know what wearing the yellow star means. "They're waiting to catch the train," he explained. "They're going to be repatriated till after the War." My heart felt suddenly lighter. That wasn't so bad, was it? It could have been a lot worse. And then my heart plummeted downwards when I heard another man laugh. "Do you really believe that?" he said. He was shaking his head. "Shameful. Quite shameful. But what can one do?"

Some people did try to do something. One woman even tried to argue with the guard. It was no use. The guard said roughly that if she didn't shut up he'd shove her on the train with all the rest. And I think it was then I knew for sure that that man had been right. They were being told a lie – to make them get on that train. And one day Jan and his whole family might be standing there, too, unless I can find a way to stop it.

Later: When I got home I told Pieter what I'd seen. "Now do you understand?" he said grimly.

"I do," I choked, swallowing back the tears that kept rising in my throat. "Piet, why do they just accept it?"

"What are they supposed to do?" Pieter said. "Where would they go? Think about it, Sis."

Usually I hate it when Pieter calls me that. But just then I didn't care what he called me. I seized his arm. "Pieter, is there nothing I can do? There must be. You *promised*."

"I told you I'll tell you when there is," he answered irritably, shaking my arm off.

There is one thing I am determined to do. Make sure Jan doesn't meet the same fate. And there may be something I can do about that.

19 JULY

I'm sure Mother knows something is up. She keeps casting worried looks at me, but I sidle away before she can ask any questions. I don't think Father notices anything though – he's simply too busy.

It's a relief when they are out. It's really only then that Pieter and I can carry on our search without anyone asking what we're doing. At least now it's the holidays I have more time. We have to be careful that our maid, Jacinta, doesn't suspect anything though. She's been with us for years but even so, I'd rather she didn't know. Looking for hiding places is what we used to do when we were children. Only then we were playing a game, and this is deadly serious.

We began our search a few days ago. Or rather, I did. Pieter had come back early and found me tapping on walls and putting my ear up close to listen. "What on earth are you doing?" he asked.

I didn't pretend. I just said: "Isn't it obvious? I'm looking for hiding places."

I had to do something and I couldn't think of anything else.

I thought he'd laugh, but he didn't. I'd almost rather he had. "I think there might be a space behind this wall. It's hollow," he said, beckoning me over to another wall.

"Even if it is, will there be room enough for someone to stand up in?"

We'll need permission before we dig into any wall. There's the attic, of course, and we have plenty of roomy cupboards where someone could hide for a time. But they'd be the first place the Gestapo would look. I haven't told Pieter why I'm doing this and he hasn't asked. But I know he doesn't need to. I know he knows.

20 JULY

Though I hate phoning Jan's house, I made myself try again. And now I know I'm not mistaken. The line is dead. I've tried three times now, dialling very slowly and carefully in case I'd dialled the wrong number. I'm trying not to panic but I can't think what this means. Will I see him tomorrow now, or not?

I've not yet found a satisfactory hiding place. There's only so long you can stand in a cupboard! And that will only fit one. Jan insists I shouldn't worry. He's spoken to his father who's told him that the whole family have an exemption. They won't be sent away. I'm eager to believe him, but I'd feel a lot happier if I knew they had somewhere safe to go.

I'd like to talk to Pieter, but his friends are round. They've turned the radio up too loudly for me to hear what they're saying – he must guess I listen at the wall. I know I shouldn't, but I feel pretty desperate. I wish he'd turn it down. The Nazis only allow certain kinds of music to be broadcast. I don't think much of it.

The news from the War is still not good, but Father says we must keep hope alive within us. Today that feels almost impossible.

21 JULY

To my relief Jan was already in the churchyard when I arrived. I told him I'd tried to phone and he said he doesn't know why the line is dead but his father is asking an engineer friend of his to try and fix it – he has plenty of time on his hands now that he's lost his business. I kept to myself this horrible feeling I have that the Nazis have cut all the Jews' phone lines. One more of their decrees. You know. *Jews are no longer allowed to make private phone calls.*

I asked him if he has many Gentile friends. He shook his head. "Not now." There was so much meaning in those two words. Then he turned to me and smiled. "Just you." I asked him what he thought about Jews and Gentiles being friends. "I think all people should reach out to each other," he said. "We're all the same underneath."

"Like this?" I said, my hand creeping towards his. Our fingers intertwined.

"Something like this." He let go of my hand to draw me closer. "More like this," he said, his face against my hair. In spite of everything I felt so at peace. Then suddenly he jumped up. "The curfew!" he exclaimed. He gave me a quick kiss, reached for his jacket, dragged it over his shoulders and bolted off.

He has further to go to get home than me. And he has to walk all the way. I pray he reaches the house in time, or his parents will be so angry. And that's if he doesn't run into the police or any Nazi soldiers first.

I think longingly of our secret garden. There it had still been possible to pretend the War wasn't happening. It's impossible now. Even our few precious moments together are cut short by the curfew.

23 JULY

Pieter has just left me. I am trying not to despair. The exemptions are worthless. They're being handed out to reassure Jews that they have nothing to fear. They might not be sent away for a long time, but they will be sent away.

I burst into tears when he told me. I felt as if I'd always known it. A Nazi do the decent thing? What had I been thinking? Pieter put his arms around me and gave me a big hug. "We'll find a place to hide him," he said.

"It's not just him," I wailed. "There's all the family, too. He won't hide if they won't."

"I know," said Pieter. "Don't you worry, I'll think of something."

I must say Pieter's been a whole lot kinder to me lately. I still worry a lot about him working for the Resistance. It's so dangerous. But I am grateful, too. Maybe he will be able to help us.

25 JULY

Pieter's face was ashen when he climbed into my room earlier this evening. I told him to sit down, while I fetched him a cup of tea. He fell into the chair, as if he was too exhausted to move. There was a smudge of oil on his cheek and his hands were dirty. I didn't like to think where he'd been or what he'd been doing. I didn't ask either. I knew he couldn't tell me.

What I poured out of the pot was almost grey. Not like tea at all. We eke out our tea leaves, reusing them again and again. So many things are rationed I forget what they are, but Mother's quick to remind me.

She was in the kitchen when I went in. "What? Another cup?" she said.

"It's for Pieter," I said. *All the studying makes him tired*, I nearly added, but felt that was going a bit far. I don't know how he finds time for studying these days. Actually I wish he would. It's hard keeping Pieter's secret and I wonder around one hundred times a day if I should. What would I do if something happened to him? Everyone knows what happens to people who are caught. The Gestapo have been picking up other people too – innocent people – and holding them hostage. They threaten to shoot them to try and stop the Resistance blowing things up. A sort of tit for tat. *If you do this, we will shoot someone.* Father is very upset – one of the hostages is a friend of his. After the War when our own government is restored I trust those pigs who run things for the Nazis will share their fate.

I took the cup upstairs. Pieter took it from me gratefully and drank it almost in one gulp.

"Better?" I asked him. He nodded but his mind seemed far away.

"What is it, Piet?" I said.

"Don't ask!" he said shortly. I was silent. Best not to say anything when he's in this mood. He got up and went into his own room and a minute later I heard a blast of hissing and crackling through the wall. The underground have their own radio station. If he turns up the dial any more the entire house will hear. But I'd far rather he fiddled with the radio than make bombs and blow things up. One of these days he's going to get caught – if he doesn't blow himself up first.

26 JULY

Jan and I have been discussing what he should do. I broke the news that the exemption was worthless as soon as I saw him.

At first he stubbornly refused to believe it. I snorted. "Since when have the Nazis kept their word? It's a lie," I insisted, "to make you believe you're safe."

He shook his head. "It's what the Council told us," he said. The Jewish Council are in charge of Jewish affairs, but so far as I can see they seem to do what the Nazis tell them to. I had to make him believe me. So I pretended Pieter knew someone in the office that organized exemptions! That seemed to shake his confidence a little and he promised me he'd tell his parents. "It will take some persuading," he said wryly. "Father has great faith in the Council!" I wish I didn't feel so certain it was misplaced.

It was a hot evening and he'd taken off his jacket and rolled up his shirtsleeves. I stroked his bare arm softly, then felt it come round me and pull me tightly to his side. I asked him what he wanted to do when he grew up. I wanted to distract him. I wanted to make him forget the present and think to the future. He looked at me with eyes that had grown so much older. "I just want to grow up," he said. I felt as if my blood had turned to ice. I seized his hand and clung on to it. I won't let them part us. I won't!

28 JULY

I've got to tell my parents my plan to hide Jan. I don't want them to open the door one day and see the whole family standing on the step! But I can't think what to say, so I keep putting it off.

The son of one of Mrs Meier's friends has got his call-up papers. I heard Mrs Meier talking about it to Mother. The family were in a terrible state. She thinks they've gone into hiding. Wisely they said nothing to their neighbours, but the street got a rude awakening yesterday when the Nazis arrived at their door in the middle of the night. They left empty-handed, of course. Am trying not to panic. Pieter snapped at me today. But I can't help worrying. A flat country like Holland has few natural hiding places and we're surrounded on all sides by Nazi-occupied countries or the sea, which is well guarded by soldiers. I don't want to wait till there's nowhere left. I'm racking my brains. Doesn't Jan's family have any Gentile friends who will be prepared to help? Jan says they have, but they don't want to put them in danger!

It's fine and honourable of them, but I wish they'd think about their children! Jan thinks they do not truly believe there is any danger. His father even thinks they might be better off if they left! I know it's been very difficult for Jewish people in Amsterdam recently. Few can have much money left now the Nazis have robbed them of most of it, and are having to sell their possessions just to be able to feed their families.

I only have to look at Jan to know that money is short. He's too proud to accept any, of course, but I'd brought him two of Pieter's old shirts. He was pathetically grateful for them. They're about the same size.

1 AUGUST

Snapped at Jan today, then immediately felt guilty. He said it was all right, but it isn't. If I feel I'm almost at breaking point what must it be like for him? I told him that if something didn't change soon, I'd go round to his house and haul out his family myself. That brought a small smile to Jan's face. I felt I could see what he was thinking. *That would go down well with Mother!*

What frightens me almost as much is that each time I see him I'm afraid he'll tell me it's over. How can a relationship like ours flourish when all we can do is sit and chat on a churchyard wall? We never used to quarrel. Each time I see him I keep fearing it will be the last.

4 AUGUST

Am so miserable. Really lost my temper today. I told Jan that if call-up papers arrived for him before they'd found a safe place to go that he must come to us. I explained that there was a secret way in, at the back. I told him exactly where it was. I said we'd hide him until we found him somewhere else. But what did he say? *"I won't leave my family."*

He won't leave his family! That was when I lost my temper. I regret it bitterly now, but I was fed up trying to persuade him. I'd done all I could. I said my brother was spending a lot of time trying to find them all a hiding place. But it seemed that we were wasting our time. I was so upset that I slid down off the wall and left him. He didn't call me back, of course. He was too afraid to shout – it might alert someone. But he's quite happy to sit and wait for the Gestapo to fetch him.

Now that I've calmed down, I feel miserable. How could I have been so unkind? It is much worse for him. He's torn between me and his family. I pull one way – them another. We'd already agreed to meet tomorrow. I just hope he's there.

5 AUGUST

Anneke came over today. A week ago, we'd agreed to meet, but this morning I rang and told her not to come. I didn't want to see anyone. I nearly broke down while trying to explain and she simply said, "I'm coming!" and put the phone down. I rubbed a wet flannel over my face. I'd been crying and didn't want her to know.

I didn't want to go anywhere, but she made me. "Trust me, you'll feel better if you do," she said. So we went out into the town, first to a café where we talked and talked. Then we went for a stroll in the park. The sunshine beamed down on us. It felt strange to do normal things again. To walk about freely. Jan and I have never been able to do that. We've never sat in a café together, or even been to the park. I found myself watching people with new eyes. Children at play, couples strolling, hand in hand. It made me feel sad. I glanced up to see Anneke's eyes on me. "Haven't you missed this?" she asked. I felt that she was trying to say, *Why are you making things so difficult for yourself. Forget him and meet someone else. Have a more normal life. You'd be a lot happier.*

"Anneke…" I began.

She seemed to read my mind. "I'm wasting my time, aren't I?"

I nodded.

"I'm glad I don't have a boyfriend," she said with feeling.

I nearly said, *You'll feel different when you meet someone you like*, but I didn't. It's the sort of thing a mother would say. Anyway who am I to preach at her? She's content and I'm not. For a fleeting moment as I looked at her I wondered if I wouldn't rather be her, happy and untroubled. But the answer came swiftly back. No, I wouldn't. Whatever happens between Jan and me, I have no regrets.

Later: I've been thinking and thinking what to do and I've made up my mind. I'm going over to Jan's house. His address is in my pocket, along with a carefully worded note. I've told Mother I'm not hungry (true) and am having an early night (not true). As soon as I put down my pen I'm going to pull up the window and climb down on to the balcony. It's only a short jump from there down to the ground. Jan didn't come to the churchyard today – and I've simply got to find out why. Is he angry with me? Is that why he didn't come? *Or – has he been called up?*

I'd made my way to the churchyard as soon as I'd left Anneke. I waited twenty minutes – twice the time we'd agreed we'd wait. I'd have waited longer but the clock was already striking half past seven. I knew he'd never come then.

I cycled home as fast as I could. In my haste I nearly knocked into someone and heard them swear at me. But I kept going. I simply couldn't control my thoughts. Visions of Nazi raids, of unanswered call-up papers, of the family being forcibly dragged from their house flooded my mind. At home I flung down my bike and flew up the stairs to my room. I paced up and down, trying to calm myself. There had to be something I could do. I rang Jan's number, my fingers shaking so much that I had to stop and dial again. But of course the line was still dead. I should have cycled straight over to Jan's house as soon as I'd left the churchyard. What had I been thinking?

There is only one course left to me. I'll be back before anyone misses me.

More when I return.

Night: I'm writing to try and distract myself. I'm back. I never got to Jan's house. There was a raid in a nearby street. I hid till the vans had gone, then I was so afraid that I ran all the way back home. Jan was wrong about me. I'm a coward.

I'd felt a bit nervous as I pulled up the window. I'd climbed out of it lots of times when I was a child, but that had been a game. This was very different. I climbed down as quietly as I could – I could hear Pieter's radio and I didn't want him to look out and see me. I patted my pocket several times, to reassure myself that I had my ID card. I didn't stop to think of course what the soldiers would say if they saw me wandering around the streets at night. I crouched down and padded over to the edge of the balcony. Then I took a deep breath and jumped. I landed softly and it didn't hurt at all.

I began to tiptoe along the street, wishing I had eyes all round my head. It was almost dark now but there was enough light still for me to see where I was. The moon was already up too and pools of shimmering light glistened on the waters of the canal. As I crept along its side I saw what I thought was the branch of a small tree reflected in the water. Then part of it moved and I realized it was the muzzle of a soldier's gun.

I crouched down, scarcely letting myself breathe. My heart swung inside me like the pendulum of a clock. At last he moved away and I was able to breathe again.

I knew I'd be safer on the side streets, so I got off the main street as soon as I could. These streets were darker – and so quiet! I could hear my feet, even my breath. And I didn't encounter any more soldiers until I was nearly at the street where I'd turn off for Jan's.

I never got there! Just as I reached the end of the street, two vans roared up. I flung myself backwards, my heart thumping wildly. The vans screeched to a halt halfway down the street. I flattened myself back against a wall, and kept as still as I could. Ahead I saw the doors of the vans open and men in the uniform of the Dutch police jumped out. If I moved now, those men might see me. I had to stay. I had no choice. Not that I could have moved if I'd wanted to – terror had glued my feet to the pavement. I watched as the men ran up to a house. One banged on the door with his rifle butt while another held down the bell. The noise would have woken anyone who hadn't already been alerted by the vans. Up and down the street windows banged shut. I could imagine the terror behind those shut windows. "Open!" I heard a policeman shout. "Open the door!" Tentatively the door opened a crack, then I saw it pushed right back and soldiers and policemen poured through. I could hear them shout, "Jood. Jood. Any Jews here?" then a few cries, voices pleading, the harsh retorts of the soldiers. Figures began to emerge slowly from the building, stumbling in the glare of the vans' headlights.

It was awful. I had to wait and watch while the vans were filled, both of them, then they roared off down the street, lights winking, and turned the corner. Now at last I managed to order my feet to move – slowly at first. Then I ran. This time I didn't bother trying to be quiet, and in those silent streets my feet pounded the pavement like an elephant's! I looked straight ahead. I had only one thought in my mind. *I must get home!* My breath came in ragged gasps. But if anyone did hear me, they were wise enough to keep inside. Every door was shut and locked, every window closed. No one would open them again until morning.

I didn't stop running till I was home. I crept round to the back of the house and climbed up on to the balcony.

My window was still open. I hauled myself through it and collapsed on to the bed. For a while, I simply lay there, trying to catch my breath, and to forbid my mind to dwell on what I had seen. It was impossible!

I was still lying there when the door opened a crack. Pieter's head peered round. He looked at me, then at the open window.

It wasn't hard for him to deduce what I'd been doing.

"You've been out?" he said. He sounded incredulous.

I nodded.

"Idiot! What were you thinking!"

I felt my face crinkle up. Honestly, I'm becoming such a cry-baby! I pulled myself together. "Pieter, I had to. Jan didn't come to our meeting place, the phone line's dead and I didn't know what else to do." Then I told him about the raid. Pieter sat down on the bed. He didn't try to reassure me. There was no point.

I thought he might say, you should have waited till morning, but instead he said: "I'll go there. Might be able to find something out."

I should have told him no. I should have said it was too dangerous. Instead I seized his arm and said: "Oh Pieter, would you?" Love makes us selfish.

Now all I can do is wait. I'm counting the minutes. It's only been ten minutes since Pieter slipped out of my window. But it seems so much longer. He should find the house easily.

I gave him very detailed directions. I'm trying to relax but my nerves are far too tightly strung for that.

6 AUGUST

Early: I'm writing by the window. There's just enough light to see. I must have been sleeping heavily because I didn't hear Pieter climb back in. He'd pulled down the window but hadn't closed the curtains and it was the early morning light that must have woken me up.

As soon as I realized he was safely back, I got up and tiptoed through to his room. I opened the door quietly. Pieter was asleep, of course. I stood there looking down at him. I couldn't wait till he woke. I had to know. I shook his arm until he muttered something and turned over in bed.

"Pieter – please tell me," I whispered. He groaned, turning on to his back and opening an eye.

"Note," he grumbled. "On the bed. Now go away!" He turned over on to his side.

I hurried back to my room. There on the end of the bed was a hastily scribbled note. Pieter must have written it before he went to bed. If I hadn't known how annoyed he'd be to be woken again I'd have gone straight back to his room and given him a big hug. How thoughtful he was being. He'd put himself in danger for me. And I'd not even managed to stay awake!

The note simply said. "All fine. Don't worry. Will tell all later."

I gulped. So amazingly he had learned something. I'll have to wait till it's really morning to find out what. But it's all right. It's all right. Pieter, how can I ever thank you enough?

Morning: This is what I have – at last – learnt from Pieter. (I know I shouldn't grumble, but I cannot understand how he manages to sleep for so long!)

He did get to Jan's house. Of course, it was dark because of the blackout, but someone in the house must have heard him creeping about because a window on the second floor opened and a head peered out.

"Could you see who it was?" I said.

He grinned. "It was Jan. Unless he's got a brother."

"Why didn't you say that you'd seen him?" I demanded.

He looked surprised. "I said everything was OK, didn't I?" (Who but a boy wouldn't understand how it mattered?) "Anyway, you were asleep." He shrugged. "And I knew that you'd want to go over and over every little thing in the morning." He pulled a face. Like girls do, I felt he was saying.

"So what happened then?" I asked.

"Well, not much actually. I said I was your brother."

"Did he come down?"

"Sort of." He grinned again. "He's got a back way out like we have. He sat out on the back roof and I told him that you were worried about him."

"Oh, Pieter!" I said, half smiling, half in tears.

"He said he was sorry about yesterday. He'll see you tonight, usual place." He gave me a look. "So stop worrying."

I said I'd try to. Then I hugged him – a lot – until he said to get off him and that I was embarrassing him.

It takes so little to make me feel happy now. But I must remember – none of our problems have been solved. Pieter still hasn't found somewhere for Jan's family to hide. But at least I know that they have a way of escaping from the house should the worst happen. And that makes me feel a whole lot better.

Evening: I've just got back from the churchyard. Jan was there, as he said he'd be. I had to stop myself from running into his arms. But that was where I apologized to him. He said he should apologize, too. He'd been an idiot. He's been thinking about things and so it seems has his father. He's now busy trying to think where they might go, should they need to – and he has hopes that an old Gentile friend might be able to shelter them for a while, until other arrangements could be made. I felt as if the sun had come out. (It's been out for days but I'd been feeling too worried and miserable to care.) Of course it may come to nothing, but the important thing to my mind is that Jan's father has at last accepted they cannot rely on the exemption.

Jan told me he often uses their back route out, when he comes to see me. I'd wondered what excuse he gave, and now I know. He doesn't.

We're meeting again the day after tomorrow. I've got to screw up my courage to face my parents. If they're part of the plan, they *have* to know. I can't put it off any longer.

7 AUGUST

I'm trying to remember what I said. I can remember what Mother said. I wish I couldn't. I don't even like writing it down. It was just as well Father came in when he did. I'd wanted to wait till Father was home, but Mother said she wanted to talk to me. She felt that we weren't communicating very well. In other words, *Are you seeing that boy? Don't you know how dangerous that could be for you both?*

I didn't know what to say. I didn't want to lie, but I didn't want her to forbid me to see him. It was my blush that told her what I couldn't.

"Oh, Katrien," she said. Then she said that she'd always brought me up to tell the truth and was very disappointed in me. She felt she had failed as a mother! And a lot more. I was too upset to know what I said, and it was then that Father walked in. His eyebrows went up.

"Why, Katrien!" he said. My face was red and hot and wet with tears.

"Father," I wept. "I'm sorry."

And then I told him everything.

He was silent for quite some time. Then he said we should all sit down and think what was the best thing to do. Mother opened her mouth to say something but Father put up his hand and she was silent. She'll listen to Father. Wish she'd listen to me!

They said they'd like to help – at least Father did. But then he said: how could they? Where would we hide him? And how would we feed him? He won't have a ration card if he's in hiding. I couldn't believe what I was hearing. And it was *Father* who was saying these things. It was what I'd expected from Mother. And he kept on finding problems. How the neighbours would find out. What would they tell Jacinta?

Problems. Problems. Problems. I couldn't understand it. We'd find a way, wouldn't we? We'd be helping someone hide from the Nazi terror. Wasn't that all that mattered?

I put my face in my hands. I'd told Jan he could come here if there was nowhere else. How can I tell him he can't?

My heart feels like a stone inside my chest. It's up to Pieter now.

8 AUGUST

I climbed out of my window to meet Jan this evening. I felt as if I was defying them. Not that I care. They haven't actually forbidden me to meet him, but they'd ask where I was going, if they saw me leave by the front door.

I cycled to our meeting place as fast as I could. I'd made up my mind. I was NOT going to tell Jan our house was forbidden to him. I told myself that in a real emergency they would let him stay. Rations? We'd manage. It'd be better if I ate a bit less, so I could fit into my winter clothes that I was already growing out of. As for Jacinta, we'd tell her not to clean the upstairs rooms. It was only for the short term – until we found him somewhere else…

But as I sat down next to Jan, I had to make a real effort to hide how worried I really was. I didn't want to spoil our precious time together. I hated leaving him. How many more times will I be able to sit by his side? Each time he holds me I think, this may be the last time. The last time *ever*. And I try to remember what it feels like, just in case…

11 AUGUST

Found a note under the door. Don't know how it got there or when. I opened the envelope with shaking hands. I recognized Jan's handwriting at once. "Gone to stay with friends. So enjoyed meeting you!"

It felt like someone had thrust a knife into my chest, it hurt so much. How could he be so cruel! Pieter found me later in my room. He said he'd heard me.

I told him to leave me, but he said he couldn't. Not in that state. In between sobs I blurted out I'd had a note. I thrust it at him. Pieter looked at it for a moment and then said: "I know why he wrote that. In case the wrong person picked it up. It's like a sort of code."

He pointed out that Jan hadn't even signed it.

"I'll go there," he said getting up. "Just to make sure. But I bet you I'm right."

I was being slow. "What do you mean?

"They'll be hiding, you nitwit."

It was a tiny scrap of hope to cling to, and I clung to it. Then I thought a bit more. "But I don't know where," I said dolefully.

"Better you don't," Pieter said.

"How can you say that?" I exclaimed.

"Think of him for once," he said shortly.

Then he left me to my tears and my pillow.

Later: Pieter is back – and insists he was right. He managed to speak to a man who was leaving the house as he reached it. *Who?* the man said. *Never heard of them. You must have the wrong address.* Pieter says it's obvious he was lying. They'll have gone into hiding. Everyone is frightened. No one will tell the truth, and certainly not to a stranger. I'm trying not to feel hurt. How long did Jan know? I don't care what Pieter thinks. He doesn't understand.

I feel as if I'm standing alone at the edge of a vast and empty wasteland – that's what my life feels like now. If only I'd told him how important he was to me when I had the chance. I'd not been brave enough. And I might never have another one.

14 AUGUST

It's awful. Each day brings news of fresh round-ups. I avoid certain parts of the city. Every night I say prayers for Jan and his family. I think about him all the time. I miss him so much. The days seem so long. Mother must have seen me moping about the house, but she probably thinks I'm sulking. Let her. I don't care what she thinks.

Later: Had to shove my diary away quickly. Mother has just been up to see me. She says she is worried about me. I said I could look after myself – thank you. She sighed and said, "It's just you're still so young, Katrien. I don't want you to be hurt."

I know she wants to protect me, but I don't want her to. I'm not a child.

I feel as if I've grown up a lot these past few weeks, even if Mother hasn't realized that yet.

15 AUGUST

Early: I've found a new hiding place for my diary, in the space between two drawers in my dressing table. It's a good thing too as I need to be even more careful now.

I began to write when Jan was asleep, but he woke up and asked me what I was doing. I shut my book quickly, so he couldn't see what I was writing, but I told him what it was.

"It's my diary," I said. He wanted to know what I wrote in it. I thought about it but in the end I just smiled. I couldn't very well say, It's about you and me.

What are Mother and Father going to think when they learn that Jan has been under their roof all night? I know I've got to tell them. I'd hoped to hide him for a few days first, but he won't let me. Of course I hadn't told him what they'd said to me. And I can't very well tell him now! I got out of bed and curled up next to him on the heap of blankets I'd given him for the night. He kissed a strand of my hair.

"In the morning," I said. "I'll tell them then." I dread it, and am willing the hours to pass very slowly. If only there was a way to seize a special moment and hold on to it, or turn the hour arm of the clock back. They will let him stay, won't they? Please, please, please! Just for a few days. Until we find him somewhere else.

It's over two hours now since Jan got here. I was in bed, trying to sleep. Next door I could hear the low hum of Pieter's transistor. Father and Mother were having an early night, too. Father is so tired these days. His list of patients seems to be growing.

I was half asleep when something woke me. A patter against the window, like tiny pebbles or a handful of gravel. At first I thought I was merely dreaming and shut my eyes and tried to sleep. But then it came again. This time I knew I wasn't. There was someone out there. I was a bit frightened. Who could it be? I knew it wasn't Pieter. I got up and pulled aside a curtain and looked out. Someone was crouching on the balcony below. He looked up. I felt my heart turn over. It was Jan.

My hands were shaking so much it was an effort to pull up the window. I'd thought I'd never see him again. Yet here he was, outside my bedroom window. Why was he here? Was he in danger? At that moment I didn't care. All I felt was happy.

I forced myself to sit down on the bed. I'd find out soon enough. In a few minutes. In a minute. In a few seconds. He was here. I held out my arms.

When we'd stopped holding on to each other, he explained. His father had found a safe hiding place for them. They'd had to leave in a hurry and could only take a few things with them. He held up his rucksack. "Everything I own is in here," he said with a wry smile. He couldn't even tell me where they were – in case someone else picked up the note. "I hoped you would understand what I was trying to say," he said. "I hated not being able to tell you the truth." I saw him swallow. "Do you forgive me?"

"Nothing to forgive," I said. But I was puzzled. Why then had he come to me? Jan explained. They'd been there only a few days when their friend told them that he was sorry, but they would have to leave. He was worried that the neighbours were growing suspicious. He found someone else who was prepared to take them in in exchange for money. But there was only room for three. Jan made the decision easy for them by creeping out at night. Then he came to me.

"I wanted to," he said. "I know I may not be able to stay, but I wanted to see you so badly. I missed you so much," he murmured, his face against mine.

I made up a bed for him on the floor. Then we sat side by side and we talked – for hours and hours. I've given up trying to sleep now. I don't even want to. I don't want to waste these precious minutes sleeping. They might be almost the last I ever spend with Jan. I keep leaning over the side of the bed to look down at him. To prove to myself I'm not dreaming. Even though I can see his sleeping shape, it's hard to believe that he's really here. If only the night would go on for ever.

Later: I did fall asleep but Jan was awake before me. He leant over me and gave me a kiss. I felt like Sleeping Beauty being woken by her prince in the fairytale. I stared up at him, almost unable to believe he was really there. As I'd struggled to stay awake I'd wondered again and again if he'd still be there in the morning. It was wonderful to find that he was.

I looked across at the clock. Nine o'clock! As late as that! I leapt hastily out of bed. It's the holidays and Mother is relaxed about my sleeping in, but any minute now she was bound to come upstairs to wake me.

Jan said he'd come down with me. I said it would be better if I talked to them first. Mother would faint away if she saw us walk downstairs together. Besides, Jacinta was downstairs. In the end Pieter said he'd go down to prepare them while I took Jan up to the attic. He'd heard us talking and immediately guessed who our nocturnal visitor was.

I sat on the top stair, heart thumping. I listened as hard as I could. Any minute now I thought Mother would come storming upstairs and throw Jan out! But all I could hear was Jacinta singing in the kitchen. I kept glancing at my watch. How long before I dared go down? The door to the dining room remained firmly shut. Finally I couldn't stand it any more. I walked slowly down.

The kitchen door was shut but I could hear Jacinta inside, still singing to herself. It was better that she didn't know about Jan. Luckily, the attic is one place she never goes unless Mother specially asks her to. It's hot and dusty and cluttered with boxes and things Mother means to get rid of but never does. For now it's the safest hiding place I can think of.

I stood outside the dining room door, taking deep breaths to calm myself. Then I pushed it open. Everyone looked up. Pieter gave me a cheerful wink. Was that a good sign? My eyes went quickly to Father's and then to Mother's face. They looked very serious. My heart sank, and I steeled myself for bad news. I'd tried not to let myself hope, but deep down I'd never truly thought they'd throw a boy out on to the street.

"Well," said Father dryly. "It seems we have another mouth to feed." I flung my arms around his neck.

"It's only for a time, Katrien. You must understand," Mother said quietly.

I nodded. Of course I did. A day. A week. What did I care? He was staying.

"He can stay until other arrangements can be made for him," said Father. "Pieter says he had to leave his hiding place because there wasn't enough room for them all." He smiled at me. "He's a very brave young man. I'm looking forward to meeting him again."

Mother looked at Father. I could tell from her expression that she didn't care how brave he was. Jan was a problem that she'd rather not have. But they've made their decision. Jan can stay. And I know my parents. I know they will look after him. For now at least Jan is safe.

I took Jan some bread and tea and the good news. He was perched on one of the boxes, and I squatted down next to him. As I told him what they'd said I could see tears in his eyes. "Your parents are good people," he said. His voice was trembling. I put the plate and cup down by him and put my arms around him to comfort him. He's been so brave. You can't be brave all the time. Now I must try and be strong for him. He's lost so much. He's had to leave his family. I can't imagine what that must feel like. I might not always see eye-to-eye with mine, but it would break my heart to have to leave them. He must wonder if he'll ever see them again.

Father and Mother went up separately to see him. Mother made him up a bed in the attic, and I took up a cushion for him to sit on and some books to read. She said she was sorry it was so dusty and untidy, but in a way that makes it a safer place for someone to hide in. She made him promise he'd hide away the bedding in a box when he wasn't using it so that if anyone did go in there there'd be no evidence for them to find. What none of us said was that in that case he would need somewhere else to hide, too. I think that's why Mother is so worried. If anyone suspects we have a secret visitor word might get out to the wrong people, and we could get a visit from the police. It's awful to write that I can't be sure who we can trust. That is something that is much on my mind.

She's made out a list of rules Jan has to obey if he's to stay here. He can only come down when we tell him it is safe. That means he will have to spend most of every day up there, for Jacinta works for us nearly every day. And if a neighbour or friend calls round he must go back up straight away. Otherwise in the evenings he may join us. But he must remember always to speak quietly. The walls of the house aren't as thin as those of many in the city, but we can't risk any of our neighbours hearing him. Mrs Meier I'd trust with my life. But on the other side lives a widow – Mrs Berger. There's just something about her that makes me feel uncomfortable. The way she looks at you, the way she wants to know everything about you. She seems to know a lot about other people, too. She may not mean any harm, but she's a terrible gossip. Mother says she's just lonely, but I'd be terrified if she ever learnt about Jan. But in spite of everything I've never felt happier. I'll be able to spend lots of time with Jan now.

17 AUGUST

Jan is desperate that his parents know that he is safe, so this afternoon I cycled over to the address he had given me. It was quite a distance from our house but it was a fine afternoon and I enjoyed the ride. I was smiling and a soldier whistled at me as I rode past. I gave him my best scowl in return.

The house on Jan's address was a small shabby one in an area I didn't know well. But at least it was quiet. I got off my bike and leant it against the wall. Then I went up to the door and rang the bell. It didn't seem to work so then I knocked. A thin sharp-nosed woman opened the door a crack. "Who are you and what do you want?" she said when I told her I had a message for her friends. A sour smell wafted past her. I tried not to step away.

"Just say it's a friend," I said.

She shook her head and tried to shut the door on me. I jammed my foot in it while I thought what to say to her. I was determined to pass on my message. "Just say this, will you?" I said. "He is all right. That's all. He is all right." She nodded and I withdrew my foot. I got back on my bicycle and cycled home fast. I wasn't smiling now – I hadn't expected a reaction like that. I told myself not to worry – she was just being careful – but if she responds like that every time a stranger comes to her door, she'll soon rouse people's suspicions.

I said nothing to Jan, except that I'd passed on the message. A look of huge relief crossed his face. I sat down next to him and gave him the cup of weak tea I'd made from leftover tea leaves. I must have sneezed around twenty times in that attic! It's a good thing Jan isn't affected like me by the dust, or I don't know what we'd do.

Pieter has been measuring dimensions by the hollow wall, tools by his side. He asked if I'd like to be carpenter's mate. So I put on my oldest clothes and tried to follow his instructions. But I failed miserably at the one task he set me so I sat down on my heels to watch. When Jacinta had left for the day, Jan came down to help. He's a lot better at this sort of thing than me. He's worked out he could even make the space big enough for *all* of us to fit in – if … but I won't let myself think about that.

20 AUGUST

I don't know how we'd manage without Mother's tins! She's always kept a well-stocked larder. Father says it's because she remembers what it was like during the last war. So when this war broke out we had lots of tins and dried foodstuffs put aside which Mother said would come in very useful. I'm beginning to find out just how useful! But the stock is running low of all the foods we actually like. And some of what's left is already out of date.

Jan's food is a worry. As he's in hiding we have to share our rations with him. Because he spends most of his time just sitting in the attic, you'd think he'd need less than the rest of us, but he's a boy, Mother said. And it's true that Pieter also has a big appetite. Pieter is going to try and get him a false ID card but it will take time – and money. Or we'll have to buy what we need on the black market, but that costs even more.

I sat with Jan in the attic for a while earlier, but it set off my sneezing again. Anyway I can't go up there often. Mother doesn't like it. She always seems to need me after I've taken Jan up his food, on the rare occasions she allows me to. It's wonderful to have him here, but I wish Mother would let us be on our own more. This evening she felt relaxed enough to let him come downstairs, but I don't think either of us enjoyed it. Neither of us felt comfortable sitting primly next to Mother and Father. Perhaps we'll get used to it in time.

21 AUGUST

This evening after supper we played a game. We were all enjoying ourselves and began to laugh, quite loudly. Then Mother went and spoilt it by putting a finger to her lips and telling us to hush. Does she really think that our neighbours would hear one extra male voice? After that Jan said he'd better say goodnight. I went into the hall with him and shut the door behind me so that for once we were on our own. I reached for him – after all we were alone – but he shook his head and said we'd better not. My parents wouldn't like it!

I watched him as he walked upstairs. Then I went back into the room. I felt a bit miserable. Father suggested another round, but I didn't feel like playing any more. I saw his eyes rest on me thoughtfully. Does he realize what a strain I'm under?

22 AUGUST

Good news! Pieter has finished building our secret hiding place and when Jacinta had gone home Jan came down from the attic to try it out. He's made it very cleverly – you'd never know there was a hiding place there. We were all impressed. Then Pieter pushed the bookcase back in front of it. It's quite heavy so that is a problem, but Pieter can just about manage to shift it.

In the evening the rest of us tried it out. Mother stepped inside reluctantly. I could tell that she absolutely hated it, and she climbed out straight away, claiming that she was claustrophobic. I didn't like it much either, but if I had to choose between hiding there or being dragged away by the Nazis and maybe shot, I think I know what I'd choose. I'm finding it hard to keep my temper with Mother. I know she wishes that Jan wasn't here. Well, then she should blame the Nazis, not direct barbed remarks at Father. *If you hadn't let Jan stay here, none of this would be necessary.* It was a good thing Jan didn't hear her. He had already gone back up to his attic.

It was Father who pointed out that one of us would need to stay outside to push the bookcase back. Before Mother could say, *I told you so*, Pieter quickly said he'd thought of that. He'd do it, then get out the back way. That was a mistake. Mother wanted to know what he meant and he had to explain about the balcony. She must have known about it. After all how did she think Jan got in? Flown through the window? He hadn't knocked on the door or rung the doorbell. That earned me another tight look.

23 AUGUST

It's Jan's birthday next week. He'll be eighteen! It sounds so grown up. I've been thinking and thinking what to give him. Freedom is what I long to give him more than anything, but no one can give him that. He doesn't complain but I know he finds it wearying spending day after day in that hot attic room. It's too warm still for a woollen jersey, but I'm knitting him one all the same. He needs warm clothes for winter. The attic is hot in summer, but icy in winter. And Jan wasn't able to bring much with him. Pieter has lent him a few of his things.

I'm sitting in my room, playing my little transistor radio quietly so that no one will hear it. It's one of the few things Jan did bring with him. It's illegal for a Jew to own one now, but Jan hid his, refusing to hand it in. He says I can keep it. I said I will keep it until he needs it again. If only the news was less gloomy. Father says at least we get the truth from London. I just wish the truth was more cheerful. (We still listen to the broadcast from London every day, but they don't want to lift Dutch spirits it seems.) Jan comes to listen too, some days. I almost wish he wouldn't. I think of him brooding over the War all alone in the attic at night. It would drive me mad. And on the evenings he can't come down, he insists I tell him every little thing the broadcaster has said. I don't, of course. I keep the grimmer news to myself. This evening when I crept up to the attic to say goodnight he took my hand and gripped it tightly, as if I was his lifeline. And in a way I think I am.

"I don't know what I'd do without you, Katrien," he said.

"You won't have to," I said.

It was almost completely dark but I swear I saw a little smile flicker over his lips. It's rare to see him smile now. It takes so little to cast him down. I'm sure I'd feel the same in his place.

24 AUGUST

Anneke phoned me this morning. "I'm back!" she announced cheerfully.

For a minute I couldn't think what she was talking about. My whole world has turned upside down over these past few weeks and Anneke seemed to be calling from a faraway place that has nothing to do with me any more. Then slowly it came back to me that she'd been to stay with relatives in the countryside. "It's been an age since I've seen you and I've lots to tell you," she said.

"I'm listening. Tell me now," I said quickly.

"I'd rather meet. Wouldn't you? It's such a long time since I've seen you. I've got heaps of news, too." She gave a giggle.

I gave in. I didn't want to hurt her feelings, but I'm in a bit of a quandary. She's bound to ask about Jan. Even if she doesn't, she knows me so well. She'll guess something is up. What *am* I going to say to her?

25 AUGUST

Just returned from my outing with Anneke. It was hard
keeping the truth from her. She's the only one of my friends
I've told about Jan, and I trust her, but even she has to be
kept out of the secret. We took a picnic to the park. I felt sure
I'd never be able to enjoy myself. But I did – a lot more than
I'd expected. It was a relief to be out of the house. It's been
difficult knowing Jan is so near and yet hardly ever being
able to be alone with him.

Picnics aren't quite what they used to be before the
Occupation but Anneke had brought a chunk of cheese back
from her aunt's, and she cut me a generous slice. When she
wasn't looking, I cut my share in half and slipped one half
into my pocket to take home to Jan. He's always hungry.

I could see that she was bursting to tell me something,
and as soon as we'd spread out the rug out it came. She's met
someone she likes. His name is Hendrik. He's a pupil at our
school, in the top class. I couldn't remember him, but she
told me he'd been staying in the same village and so she'd got
to know him. As she talked about him – all the things they've
done together, all the fun they've been having – I began to

feel more and more miserable. At last she stopped talking, and looked at me. "Is something the matter?" she asked.

"No, no," I said quickly. I made myself smile. I was being selfish. I was thinking only of myself. "Anneke, I'm pleased for you. I really am."

"It's Jan, isn't it?" she said. "Oh, I'm sorry, Katrien. I've been so thoughtless. It must be hard."

I was pulling at the grass with my fingers. "It's all right," I said.

That was all she said. I was enormously relieved. My expression must have convinced her that I didn't see him any more.

I wish I could confide in her, but I can't think when I'll be able to do that. There is only one place left to me to confide in now. My diary. I can't imagine what I'd do without it. It's not the same as being able to talk to a friend. But it's some comfort knowing there is somewhere I can put down just how I feel.

School begins again next week. I'd not been looking forward to it, but now I'm actually rather relieved.

26 AUGUST

Today was Jan's birthday. We celebrated it out on the balcony below my window. Mother wouldn't have liked that, but Jan was going crazy stuck in the hot and airless attic. He told me it was a much easier climb down to my balcony than to his flat roof. That was what he'd had to do of course when he'd sneaked out secretly to see me. It seems our mothers have a lot in common. Neither of them like us seeing each other.

He said it was amazing being outside again. It made him feel almost free. When he said that I felt like crying. I can't imagine what it must be like to spend day after day cooped up, and in constant fear that your hiding place will be discovered. I stared up into the darkening sky. If only we had wings and could fly away together. We'd cross the Channel to England. They don't persecute Jews there.

We sat down on a rug side by side. I knew we were quite safe. No one would see us, unless Pieter was in his room, and he wasn't. The only other place where we could be seen was from the house opposite and that has been empty for years. I'd managed to get another message to his family – and this time I even got one back. I was able to give it to him today. Jan said he knew the woman was a bit peculiar but his Mother wrote that she had a heart of gold – like my family, he added politely.

It was the best birthday present I could give him – though I told him I had another one for him too, and I gave him the jumper I'd been knitting. It's for next winter, I said. Jan tried it on to see if it fitted him. He kept it on until I told him to take it off. He looked as if he was about to expire! I'd made him a little cake, too! One candle on the top. He blew it out and I reminded him to make a wish. He shut his eyes so long I wondered what he was wishing. I even asked him, but he just blushed and looked embarrassed.

I was sad when it was time to go back inside. I don't think we'll be able to go out there very often, but I was glad I'd been able to give him a treat for his special day.

30 AUGUST

I don't like writing what I'm writing now, but I have to set it down. I am petrified that Jan will be discovered. We've just returned from tea at our neighbour's. Mrs Berger lives alone, in a small apartment in the house next door to us. I don't like it. It has a stale and musty smell, as if she never opens a window. We had tea in her dining room. There was a thick film of dust on the table. Perhaps she didn't notice but it put me off my food. I sat down on one of the stiff-backed chairs. As soon as I did it wobbled, so after that I sat as still and straight as I could so I didn't end up on the floor.

On the table was placed half a cake. She cut me a thin slice. "We must make it last, mustn't we?" she said, giving a little tinkling laugh, and laying it on my plate. As soon as I bit into it I nearly spat it out. It tasted as if it had been baked before the War. The last one. I nibbled it politely, drowning the taste as best I could with big gulps of tea.

I let the grown-ups talk while I pretended to listen. But my mind was on other things. I'd left my window open for Pieter to crawl back in. He'd said he'd be back before we went out for tea, but he wasn't.

"Katrien!" I dragged my mind back to the present. Mother was nodding at me and frowning. Mrs Berger had got to her feet. "Would you help me make some more tea?" she said. I got up obediently and followed her into the kitchen. I watched while she poured water into the kettle, and put it on to boil, averting my eyes from the squalor – the grimy surfaces and dirty dishes piled in the sink. A cat was sitting in a pile of unironed washing. She began to chat, about inconsequential things. Then she asked if I was still enjoying school. And if I'd had a good holiday. The sort of things grown-ups always ask. I smiled and chatted back, while we waited for the kettle to boil. Then she told me to fill up the pot and while I was doing so, she began to ask some really odd questions. How nice it was that I had a new friend. Had I known him long? And did he go to my school?

I was so startled that I nearly dropped the kettle and some boiling water dribbled on to my hand. I winced with pain. I ran my hand under the cold tap to soothe it while Mrs Berger clucked and apologized and asked if I was all right. We took the tea back in, and I drank my second cup almost in one gulp. I was desperate to leave. The relief I felt when Mother at last stood up to go!

I said nothing to Mother until we got home. Then she asked what had happened to my hand. There was a red burn on it. I said I'd spilt boiling water over it. I told her how it happened, and what Mrs Berger had said.

Mother simply nodded, but she looked thoughtful and later I saw her talking quietly to Father. I am sure it was about Jan. Does she share my fear that Mrs Berger knows we have a secret guest? We must find Jan a new hiding place – and soon.

3 SEPTEMBER

I'm lying in bed, trying to still the beating of my heart. They've gone, I tell myself. They've gone. And I feel certain that they won't be back – but I'll explain why I think that later.

After they'd left we sat in a huddle around the kitchen table. Father poured out the tea. Mother tried to, but her hands were shaking so much that she poured more hot tea on to the table than into our cups. I am thankful that Father is able to remain calm. Jan took his tea up to the attic. I got up to go, too, but of course Mother called me back.

What made them come here? Had someone seen Jan? I blame Mrs Berger – her prying questions, her eyes that seem to be able to see through walls. I'd rather blame her than myself for allowing Jan to sit out on the balcony on his birthday. But surely no one could have seen him there then. Not even Mrs Berger!

But the raid has made it even more urgent we find Jan a new hiding place. Father thinks it's unlikely they'll be back, but Mother wants him gone. *She cannot cope with the strain any longer. She never wanted him here in the first place. She had agreed, but only for a short time. But enough is enough.*

Even Father hasn't been able to change her mind. "I won't be able to sleep until he's gone," she said firmly. He's putting her family in danger. End of discussion.

I'm trying to understand. I'm trying not to hate her. She is my mother. I tell myself she just wants to protect her family. I just wish she saw Jan as part of that family. Father says it is simply her reaction to her ordeal. She will feel differently in the morning. I don't think so. We will have to find Jan a new hiding place. Though after what happened tonight, I'd say he is safe enough here – whatever Mother thinks.

It was late when the bell rang. Loud and insistent. Just like it had the day I'd seen the vans draw up near Jan's street. Only this time, it was our house! And it was we who were hiding a fugitive. I didn't dare let myself think what would happen if they found him. We'd rehearsed many times what to do in an emergency like this. Jan had heard the bell and came straight downstairs. Father and Pieter pushed aside the big bookcase that concealed the secret hiding place. We'd discussed before whether Jan should climb out on to the balcony and let himself down on to the ground but there wasn't time now. Besides, they might catch him before he could get far enough away. While I waited, I glanced out of one of the windows at the front of the house. I got a huge shock! There were guns trained on our house! A voice through a loudspeaker warned us to keep away from the windows. The Nazis are nothing if not thorough.

Jan climbed in then I helped Pieter push the bookcase back into position while Father walked downstairs to let the soldiers in before they broke the door down. The bookcase was heavy – we could only push it slowly and we tried to do it quietly. The soldiers were banging on the door too, now. Mother, Pieter and I remained upstairs. I couldn't bring myself to look at Mother. I felt awful – simply awful. It was because of me Jan was here. Because of me soldiers were going to search our house. My fault that we were terrified half out of our wits.

Their voices carried up to me, as loud and insistent as the bell.

"*Sind sie Juedisch?*"

"*Nein*," I heard Father say firmly.

"ID, please."

The soldiers began to spread out. One stayed downstairs – they must know it was unlikely anyone would hide so near the door – while the rest pounded up the steep narrow stairs to the first floor. "Any Jews here?" a voice called up. I nearly jumped out of my skin. I recognized that voice at once. It was Kurt. I stared at him as he climbed up on to the landing but he didn't give even the tiniest hint he'd ever seen me before.

"*Sind sie Juedisch?* Are there any Jews here?"

"*Nein*," we replied.

"ID, please." We gave him our ID cards and he quickly flicked through them, and handed them back.

The soldiers were about to climb up to the next floor when to my surprise Kurt put up a hand. "Leave this to me," he said. "Wait for me downstairs."

"If anyone can find a Jew Kurt will," one said laughing, as if it was a joke. At that moment I hated them, really really hated them.

The soldiers clattered back downstairs. Kurt slowly climbed the stairs to the next landing. Whatever checks he made they were quick. Perhaps he knew where to look, all the tricks, all the vain attempts people made to conceal that someone was hiding in their home.

It was only when he was walking back down to us that I noticed something I hadn't before. The bookcase that concealed the opening to Jan's hiding place wasn't quite straight. If I'd only realized while Kurt was upstairs we could have pushed it back. We'd been in too much of a hurry. Anyone taking a good look at it might wonder why and investigate further – especially if they'd had a tip-off that there might be Jews hiding in the house.

My heart began to pound. What would we do if Kurt noticed? I tried not to look at it. His eyes met mine. I knew then that he'd seen it. Knew what it concealed. But to my utter astonishment he didn't go over to look at it. Instead he went into my bedroom. He pulled up the window and looked out. He'd left the door open and I saw him flash his torch down below at the balcony. My eyes followed the beam as it travelled slowly along the wall opposite. He switched it off, and came back on to the landing.

Pieter glanced at me. He looked as mystified as me. The search Kurt was making was far from thorough.

"All seems in order. I am sorry for troubling you." He clicked his heels together and clattered back down the stairs. I heard the door slam, then the sound of the van revving up. Only when I could no longer hear it did I go over to the bookcase and help Pieter heave it back to let Jan out.

I cannot get my head round what happened here this evening. I am beginning to think that Kurt did not want to find anyone. Maybe it is a job he dislikes. Maybe it is a favour to me? But why? The few times I've encountered him I've been barely civil to him.

It is a mystery, and one I will probably never be able to answer.

4 SEPTEMBER

Father has managed to persuade Mother that Jan can stay – for now. But now Jan's been threatening to leave!

This morning when I took him his breakfast I found him pacing up and down. He jumped when he heard me. I'm not surprised. After last night, I'd be terrified every time I heard someone climb up the stairs.

"It's only me," I said, putting the tray down.

He didn't pick it up. His eyes when they met mine were strained and anxious.

"Katrien, look," he said. "I can't stay here. I feel terrible knowing the danger I've put your family in."

What was he talking about? To me, he was part of the family. But I didn't say it.

"Don't worry. I'm sure they won't come back now." My heart was lurching inside me, but I tried to hide how I felt.

"You can't be sure."

"Yes, I can. Besides, where would you go?"

He sat down and I squatted down next to him. "Do you remember my telling you about the man who pulled me away from the police?" he said. I nodded. "Well, I've been thinking, maybe he'd be able to help."

It's one thing hiding someone from the police for a few minutes, quite another sheltering them for a long time, I thought, but we were both so desperate that I simply said, "Sounds a good idea. I'll go and see him after school today."

He seemed relieved and was actually able to eat his breakfast. I sat there with him till he'd finished and then took the tray downstairs to the kitchen. Jacinta had gone out on an errand, so I didn't have to worry about her.

I just hope he won't do anything rash. But before I went

to school I left Pieter strict instructions to bar my window to him – just in case!

Later: This afternoon I took the tram across town. I felt as if I was embarking on a desperate mission, the success of which I felt very doubtful, but I'd promised Jan. Besides, what else could I do? I'd memorized the address he'd given me. I said it to myself over and over again – so I wouldn't forget it. I hadn't dared write it down in case I was stopped and searched for any reason.

My emotions were in turmoil as the tram deposited me at the end of the street where Jan had been chased by the soldiers. That day we'd nearly lost each other – and the fear of loss had driven us into each other's arms. I clung on to that.

I turned into the street, trying not to walk too fast. I'd brought a shopping basket with me, so people would think I was merely out shopping. The queues at the shops seem to have got longer and I pitied the poor Jewish people – having to wait till three in the afternoon to do their shopping when many of the shops have run out of what they need.

Before I'd set off I'd shown Pieter the name and address Jan had given me. I explained how the man had helped Jan, when he'd been chased by the soldiers. Pieter had pulled a face and said seriously don't ever tell our parents about *that*. They'd not want to know all this. I said it had been a simple case of Jan forgetting his ID card. Not that anything is that simple now. But I knew Pieter was right. Mother would have a fit! I asked him if he knew anything about him. He shook his head. But there are so many different Resistance cells, he said. He may be in the Resistance or he may not. It was worth a try though.

Anything was worth a try, I thought. And if he'd saved Jan once … then maybe – just maybe – he'd help him again. Frankly, I didn't know what else to do.

I looked up to see that I'd reached the house. It took a lot of courage to knock on the door. Then I had to wait. It was one of the worst waits of my life, and it seemed to go on for ever. At last the door swung open. A young man was standing there. He gave me a keen look. "Who is it wants me?" he asked. He had a pleasant face and I immediately felt I could trust him, but to test him, I gave a false name – a Jewish-sounding name. I wanted to see how he'd react. I wasn't taking much of a risk as I only had to produce my ID card, which was safely tucked into my pocket. He took my arm and pulled me inside quickly. "You should not stay in the street," he said. I saw his eye wander over my jacket. I wasn't wearing a yellow star, of course. That must have puzzled him, but I'd heard about Jews who refused to wear it. I expect he had, too.

He pulled out a chair and told me to sit down. "Now," he said. "Why have you come here? Do you need help?"

"It's not for me, it's for a friend," I said. "You helped him once before," and I reminded him of the occasion he'd pulled Jan away from the police. He listened intently. He said he remembered and I believed him. After all, how many times do you find yourself hauling boys off the street? I thought again just how lucky Jan had been. After that he asked me a barrage of questions, which I answered as well as I could. Then he looked at me for a long time. I tried to look straight back. His eyes were probing mine, testing me: *Who is this girl, and can I trust her?* So I told him the truth. "I'm not Jewish," I said.

He smiled. "I wondered when you'd tell me," he said. Then he paused, considering me again.

"We may be able to do something," he said. He went to his desk and wrote something down. "Memorize this name and address." He handed me a piece of paper. "He may be able to help you. You have come just in time. For now, I can say no more. Be very careful who you share this information with. Many lives depend on it." He gave me a serious look.

I nodded. "You have my word."

He took my hand in his and shook it. I liked the feel of it. It felt solid and trustworthy. "Goodbye – and I wish you and your friend the best of luck," he said, using an English expression.

"Thank you," I said.

Could he tell how much gratitude there was in those two simple words?

All the way home I recited the name and address in my head. As soon as I got inside I ran up to the attic and told Jan the good news. Pieter was sitting with him. "What did you say the name was?" he asked. When I told him, he became quite excited. "Eureka! I've heard that name before!" he exclaimed, jumping up and walking excitedly up and down until I had to beg him to sit down. Jacinta was dusting the upstairs bedrooms. Did he want her to hear, too? The man had already been in prison once for his work in the Resistance, Pieter told me. He was a master forger and there was more, though Pieter refused to say what. I wish I could write his name, but I've already written more than it's safe to. It would be dreadful if anyone found it and read it. I'd never forgive myself.

18 SEPTEMBER

I've been staring at my clock. Its slow tick-tock makes me want to scream. Time is moving inexorably towards some time I'd rather not think about. If only I could turn the hands forward to some time after the War. Instead time is moving fast towards something else. The day of Jan's departure. I dread it. But it is Jan's best hope, I keep telling myself. He is lucky. Things are getting worse for the Jews. A lot worse. Day by day more Jewish people are being rounded up and sent away. I should be glad for him. And I am, I tell myself. I *am*.

But what if the plan fails? What if they are stopped by the police? They have a very long way to go. It only needs one policeman to question one ID card…

I must keep these awful thoughts out of my mind.

I should be glad for him. It is our best hope now.

20 SEPTEMBER

Morning: I could hardly recognize the boy in the young man who a few minutes ago was standing in front of me. His hand in mine felt rougher, there is stubble on his chin, and he wears workman's dress. In his pocket is his ID card – a new one. But he is and always will be Jan to me.

So much has happened these past days that I didn't dare confide to my diary. But today, in a few hours' time, Jan will creep out of my window, jump to the ground and make his way to the rendezvous. There, he will join a band of men all going to labour on the Atlantic Wall that the Nazis are building.

That is his alibi. That is what they will tell the soldiers at checkpoints.

Instead I see him walking, always walking, across the land and into France, where the French Resistance will take care of them. Then they will move south to Spain – and safety. I am trying to imagine how long it will take, how soon before I can stop worrying about him. Never, I think. Never till I see him again. But one day I will. Stories can have happy endings, can't they? Even one like mine and Jan's.

Afternoon: If you're sending someone off to war, you can stand and wave. At the station. Outside the house. Or on the street, like the Dutch Fascists did to my disgust the day German and Dutch soldiers marched side-by-side, like allies, to fight the Russians, in Soviet Russia. You do not have to hide. You can throw flowers at them, hug them and wish them well, drape garlands round their necks.

I couldn't do that. I said my last farewell to Jan secretly outside my window. I'd already said it once, but as he climbed down on to the balcony he looked back up at me. I couldn't bear it. I climbed out of the window quickly and almost fell into his arms. His cheek felt rough against my smooth one, but he was still the same boy I'd met months ago. We clung to each other and then he gently put me from him. I said, desperately: "You will remember."

I didn't have to say any more. I know he will.

I stood there watching, while he climbed down to the ground. He looked back at me once more, then he quickly turned away and slipped round the side of the building where I couldn't see him any more.

I don't know how long I sat there, my arms round my knees. But then a wind whipped up, and I began to shiver. There's a touch of autumn in the air, though the sun is shining.

Mother is laying the table for tea. Mrs Meier is coming over to join us. But first I must go up to the attic and take away the blankets, the pillows, the cushion and the book that Jan was reading.

He said he'll finish it when he comes back. I'll keep it for him, the page marked where he had to stop. He said it's a good story. I'll put it next to my diary.

I've made a promise to myself. I'm going to close my diary now and I won't write another word in it. Not until Jan comes back. After all what would I write? This diary is the story of Jan and me. So I'll put it aside – just for now. He'll come back. I know he will. He promised me he would.

MY LAST ENTRY – 21 JUNE 1948

I have one more thing to write, before I put down my diary for good.

I will set it down now. I will write it exactly as it happened. I'd dreamed of this moment many times. It didn't happen quite like that. But things never happen quite the way they do in dreams.

This afternoon we had a visitor. I heard the bell ring, but I didn't take any notice. I was immersed in my book.

"Katrien!"

I got up reluctantly. I'd reached an exciting part in the story and didn't want to put it down. I'd learnt years ago – when we were still living under Nazi Occupation – how books can help you escape. At least for a time.

"Katrien," my mother called again. Her voice was full of smiles. "Come! Come quickly."

I run down the stairs. It must be something important. Mother is beaming up at me. She isn't alone. There is someone standing next to her. A young man. He looks like someone I used to know.

He looks at me for a long time without speaking.

"Hello, Katrien," he says at last.

I walk slowly up to him.

His eyes are like the sky on a summer's day. Only one person in my world has eyes like that.

I take his hand in mine. "Hello, Jan," I say.

HISTORICAL NOTE

When the Second World War broke out in September 1939, the Netherlands hoped to remain neutral. But on 10 May 1940, blatantly ignoring Dutch neutrality, German tanks rolled across the border. Ill-prepared and ill-equipped the Dutch were no match for the Nazi "Blitzkrieg". On 15 May, following heavy aerial bombardment of the Dutch city of Rotterdam, the Dutch surrendered to spare other Dutch cities a similar fate. The government and royal family escaped to Britain, where they set up a government in exile and maintained communication with the home country through secret broadcasts via the BBC in London.

Jews, many of whom had settled in the Netherlands to escape Nazi persecution in Germany, were terrified. Sea ports were crowded by Jews vainly hoping to escape by ship to Britain. Few managed to. Some even committed suicide rather than again face the Nazi terror.

In the Netherlands a new government was set up, headed by Reichskommissar Arthur Seyss-Inquart, an Austrian Nazi. Reporting directly to Hitler, Seyss-Inquart was charged with maintaining close economic ties with Nazi Germany. Sharing

Hitler's anti-Semitic beliefs, he began to dismiss Jews from government, the press and from other important positions. A programme of Nazification was to infect every area of Dutch life. The Nazis tried to isolate the Netherlands from the outside world. Maintenance of public order and security was a high priority. Everyone over fifteen years old had to register and carry an identity (ID) card, bearing their photograph, signature and fingerprints. Those carried by Jews were stamped with a "J". It was difficult to avoid registration and many essentials could not be obtained without one. But there was a more sinister motive for registration than straightforward organization of the population. Registration made it simple for the Nazis to round up Jews and deport them, a process which began in earnest in summer 1942. But in the early days of the Occupation life for most people continued much as it had done before the War. The German occupiers tried to maintain a friendly and conciliatory attitude to the general population.

Early in 1941 the mood changed. Following attacks on Jews by members of the WA – the military wing of the Dutch Fascist Party, the NSB – young Jews formed themselves into commando-style gangs to protect themselves. The Nazis retaliated to the fighting that ensued by cordoning off the Jewish Quarter with a high security fence and establishing a Jewish Council to maintain order. Then, when the Germans were attacked at a Jewish ice-cream parlour, the Nazis went a step further. In late February around 420 young Jews were deported to Mauthausen and Buchenwald concentration camps. Only two were to survive.

The measures against the Jews, and the enforced labour drafts of young Dutch to Germany outraged the Dutch and a general strike was organized in Amsterdam. The strike quickly spread to other Dutch cities and towns. Taken by surprise by the scale of the protest the Nazis reacted quickly and harshly. Several strikers were shot, others arrested and later executed. The harshness of German reprisals made people realize that public protest was futile. Resistance to the enemy occupiers became more covert. Underground presses published and secretly distributed newspapers, forgers created new identity cards for people who needed to go "underground" and safe places were found for Jews and young Dutch hiding from deportation or the labour draft. Saboteurs blew up means of communication like railway lines and telegraph poles.

Resistance was of course highly dangerous – both for the resister and their family. In other measures to stamp out resistance, the Nazis took people hostage and executed them as retaliation for an act of resistance.

Nazification touched every aspect of Dutch society. All references to the Dutch royal family were forbidden, the word "royal" was removed from public places and organizations, and the Queen's head erased from postage stamps.

Propaganda – shown on cinema newsreels and on posters plastered round the towns and cities – denounced the old government, praised the Nazis' achievements and tried to encourage people to believe that Nazi final victory was inevitable.

Nothing escaped Nazi attention. Films and music, radio programmes, reading matter, newspapers – all were censored. American, British and French films were forbidden. The only radio station the Dutch trusted for news of the War was "Radio Orange", which broadcast secretly from London. All political parties, except for the NSB, were suppressed. In schools German became the principal foreign language. In the late summer of 1941 all Jewish children had to attend separate Jewish schools.

In 1942 the Jews were made to wear the infamous yellow star. Some refused to do so, but those caught were severely punished. Other anti-Jewish measures quickly followed. By this time many Jews had lost their means of livelihood, their businesses had been given to non-Jewish owners, and now they had to obey a special curfew, shop at certain hours, their phone lines were cut, public transport forbidden them, all places of entertainment, hotels and restaurants, parks, pools, and the beach out of bounds to them. In what was to become known as the "Final Solution" the Nazis set in place plans to deport all Jews from the Netherlands (and other occupied countries). To make the process of deportation easier, the Germans began to centralize the Jews in Amsterdam where most of the country's Jews lived. In July, the first deportations began. At first many Jews did not realize what was in store for them. Their lives had become progressively more difficult. Many believed that they would be better off wherever it was they were being sent. Postcards, purporting to be from friends and relatives in the camps, helped lull them into a false sense of security. Some, for instance those working in industries essential for the German war effort, were granted special exemptions from deportation. But this merely delayed the inevitable. Raids were stepped up to winkle Jews out of hiding. Many protested about the deportations – people like church ministers and other public figures. Brave people like these were often arrested and imprisoned for speaking out. Many Jews chose to go into hiding. Others remained and obeyed the call-up, not wanting to put their families and Gentile friends in danger by going into hiding. Nevertheless many brave Dutch people risked their lives to help those hiding from Nazi persecution. Some were betrayed. It was not easy finding a place to hide and escape was very difficult. The coast was heavily fortified and the Netherlands surrounded on all other sides by countries occupied by the enemy. Some escapes were achieved, however. One such was led by the Dutch resistance fighter, Jaap Penraat, who in a number of daring expeditions led groups of young Jewish men safely out of the country under the pretence that they were slave labourers hired to work on the Nazis' Atlantic Wall fortification. But few were to be so fortunate. Of 140,000 Jewish people living in the Netherlands in 1939 only around 21,000 were to survive the War.

As the War slowly turned against the Nazis the sufferings of the Dutch people intensified. Severe food and fuel shortages meant that many were to starve in the final winter of the War. The Allies reached the Dutch border in September 1944 but it took several months of bitter fighting before the Germans were finally forced to surrender on 5 May 1945, bringing the Occupation to an end.

LOOK OUT FOR

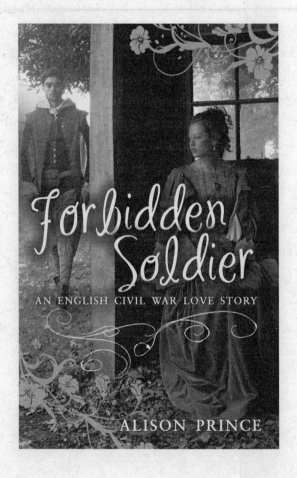